Richard Wyatt

Varieties in verse

Consisting of new metrical translations from Greek, Latin, Italian, and German

authors

Richard Wyatt

Varieties in verse
Consisting of new metrical translations from Greek, Latin, Italian, and German authors

ISBN/EAN: 9783337234249

Printed in Europe, USA, Canada, Australia, Japan

Cover: Foto ©Andreas Hilbeck / pixelio.de

More available books at **www.hansebooks.com**

VARIETIES IN VERSE;

CONSISTING OF

New Metrical Translations

FROM GREEK, LATIN, ITALIAN, AND

GERMAN AUTHORS ;

WITH COPIOUS NOTES, AND SOME ORIGINAL PIECES

By Richard Wyatt, B.A.

FORMERLY OF CORPUS CHRISTI COLLEGE, CAMBRIDGE.

DEDICATED, BY PERMISSION, TO THE LORD BISHOP OF LINCOLN.

RIVINGTONS,

London, Oxford, and Cambridge.

1869.

PREFACE.

IN presenting this Volume to my Readers, I am
desirous of stating the circumstances which led
to the production of the little work which forms the
principal part of the miscellany; and, moreover, of
adding a few words in vindication of my choice of
rhymic metre, in preference to blank verse.

In consequence of my retirement from the daily
duties of a public function which had for many years
occupied a considerable portion of my time, I found
myself in possession of more leisure than was
desirable for the promiscuous reading and other
recreations which had previously filled up my vacant
intervals; and therefore I thought it expedient to
impose upon myself some unoppressive intellectual
task, in order to ward off any *ennui* which, otherwise, I might sometimes feel. How, for this purpose,

I came to think of a new translation of the Iliad
I am unable to recollect; but that poem in the
original having, though a long time ago, formed one
of the subjects of examination for my B.A. degree,
I flattered myself to be capable of estimating the
respective merits of the only translations with which
I was acquainted; and of exercising a tolerably
correct judgment in bringing forth a new one.

To a man far advanced in life, as I then already
was, the admonition,

Vitæ summa brevis spem nos vetat inchoare longam,

might have appeared emphatically applicable in such
a case; and it would unquestionably have deterred
me from an obligatory undertaking of such magnitude; but to the extent of the first two books, at
the least, I was resolved to go; and this for two
reasons : first, because I thought that so much of
the work would test my aptitude for the task,—
inasmuch as the second book contains the most
crabbed and difficult passages to manage, with
regard both to metrical arrangement and to rhyme;
and, secondly, because those two books together
constitute a complete stage of the poem. Arrived
at this point, the reader has become acquainted with

the origin and the object of the war, and with the intestine discord in the Grecian camp which for a time impeded its success, while he sees the event of it foreshadowed; and at the end of this stage he leaves the two armies on the field of battle, ready for the great conflict.

Having proceeded thus far with my task, I began to feel that to pursue it farther would be to convert what had been a pastime into a toil.

Of all the English versions of. Homer which, up to this time, I had ever seen, the only ones were those of Pope and Cowper; the first being, as is universally known, a paraphrase rather than a translation; and the other, although a sufficiently close translation, being in blank verse; whereas I had resolved that mine should be in rhyme. Lord Derby's I, from information, knew to be in blank verse, but I had, till the period last referred to, refrained from reading it; because, on the one hand, I would not be, however unconsciously, indebted to it for aid, nor, on the other hand, be discouraged by its reputed excellences.

Both Cowper and the Earl of Derby are zealous champions for rhymeless verse; but while (to use the language of Seneca) *multum magnorum virorum*

plead guilty, but beg leave, in alleviation of judgment, to add that my limping lines are not numerous, compared with those which limp not. The truth is, that not one of them all escaped me; they are all made such with a wilful intention [!]. In poems of great length there is no blemish more to be feared than sameness of numbers, and every art is useful by which it may be avoided. A line, rough in itself, has yet its recommendations. It saves the ear the pain of an irksome monotony, and seems even to add greater smoothness to the others."

Now is not this an argument against the necessity of couplets running exactly parallel with the sense? Yet more—in favour even of the designed intro-duction into them, occasionally, of short medilinear breaks or pauses? These in rhymic verse are, as I humbly submit, quite as desirable, by way of relief to monotony, as " limping lines " are in blank verse.

The fact that the ancient poets were strangers to rhyme is not an argument (which it has been alleged to be) for yielding the preference to blank verse in English poetry (especially translations)—no, not even in long poems. For the neglect of rhyme by the ancients there was an obvious reason, if not an absolute necessity, in the structure of the Greek and Latin languages. The variety of their terminations allowed such a deranged collocation of words as would be quite impracticable in the metre of modern languages, whether rhymic or rhymeless. Even their shortest compositions (Martial's Epigrams for example) are rhymeless; and this shows that the distinction between long and short pieces, with regard to rhyme, which some moderns would establish, did not enter into the consideration of the ancients; the inaptitude of their language for such embellishment being alone a sufficient cause for its absence.

Notwithstanding " the shackles of rhyme," in their exemption from which the blank-verse poets feel, or affect to feel, so much complacency (if indeed it is not in some cases a cloak for indolence), I am bold enough to challenge a comparison with them for fidelity, clearness, and rhythm; and I hope that any candid reader who may think it worth while to make such comparison will be of the opinion that my pretensions, so far, are not ill founded.

My greater diffuseness is owing chiefly to the occasional interpolation of a gratuitous line or two

—though sometimes more,—but always in harmony with, if not also in elucidation of the context; from which, moreover, they are either' actually distinguished by italic type, or distinguishable without such aid; whereby they resemble distinct and separate *strata*, rather than unanalyzable *fusion;* while some of them may be regarded as incorporated notes.

As a set-off against this transgression, if such it be considered, I must observe that nowhere have I taken such liberties as more terse translators have done; by, for instance, substituting apostrophe for direct narration :—thus telling certain places in Greece that they, those places, instead of the troops they sent, were at Troy—

> " Thou wast also there
> Medeia, and thou Nissa: nor be thine,
> Though last, Anthedon, a forgotten name—"

or by translating ζαθέη, " lovely " (instead of *very divine* or *sacred*), as in the instances where Νίσσαν τε ζαθέην (*and very divine Nissa*) is rendered " and the lovely site of Nissa," and Κρίσσαν τε ζαθέην, " Crissa's lovely plain."

I have been driven to the making of these perhaps apparently cynical, but really good-tempered, remarks, by the somewhat arrogant claims and exultant tones of the anti-rhymers.

Since the cessation of my task, I have compared its result with the florid paraphrase of Pope; with the almost faithful, and, in many parts, very agreeable translation of Cowper, *malgré* his boasted lame lines; and also with the "fair and honest" (to adopt his own character of it) version of the Earl of Derby [1]; and in neither the first nor the last of these versions have I found a single line quite corresponding in diction with one of my own; while in Cowper's I have discovered only one entire line in common between us; and that one so composed, and so close to the original, as not to have admitted of variation (had it been attempted) without wilful distortion; which, moreover, could not have been effected but at the expense of discomposing and reconstructing several neighbouring lines.

In this result I have gratified a curiosity which had operated with me as a secondary or auxilliary motive for this undertaking; that, namely, of ascertaining how different persons, working in-

---

[1] This character is permitted to remain, notwithstanding Mr. Edwin Arnold, in his recent work on " the Poets of Greece," ventures to say, " Lord Derby's over-praised edition wants every thing which a translation should have, except good intentions."

dependently on the same material, might at once differ and agree; and it is interesting to observe how extensively variety of phraseology may consist with identity, or at least similarity of ideas and sentiment; thus affording an exhibition of the ductility of language, with the idiosyncrasies of thought.

As yet I have said nothing about the minor translations and original pieces, which are added as a make-weight to the principal article. They were composed at different periods, and not in a chronological order corresponding to their local arrangement.

My translations of portions of the sixth and twenty-fourth books of the Iliad, which appear in company with Pope's and Cowper's version of the same passages, were made some months later than the foregoing; and the reasons for that accompaniment appear with it.

In printing a translation of parts only of the Iliad, I plead the precedent of the nobleman above named, who originally published one only of his books of it—among other " Translations of Poets Ancient and Modern." While thus so far following his example, I wish I could approach his merits without, at the same time, coveting the nobility which might cover a multitude of imperfections.

The last sentence was written on the night of Saturday, the 23rd of October; and with it I suspended my lucubrations for that evening; all unconscious of the mournful fact that in the morning of the same day the powerful and polished mind of that great man had passed away!

The remarks on his work which I have made here and in my notes, which had several weeks previously gone to the press (and which I should have been willing for his lordship to see, had his life been spared), I find no reason for cancelling or altering, now that he is gone.

In the full consciousness that I cannot long survive him, I hasten to the conclusion of this my final task. In doing so, I shall change the first for the third person, and add:—If in the limited circulation of this book (which is not intended for *publication* in the full and conventional sense of the term) a copy of it should stray into the sanctum of some Apollo, among the awful fraternity of literary deities ycleped Reviewers; and he, instead of assuming his character of Phœbus, and so shedding his benign rays upon the production, should prefer acting in his other character of Smintheus, he may be assured that, however much his arrows may damage the offspring, they cannot προϊάπτειν the parent to the shades.

CONTENTS.

THE ILIAD.

Book I

G ODDESS of song, in tuneful strains rehearse
⎯ Achilles' wrath, fierce, lasting, and perverse ;
Which woes immense on the Achæan band
Inflicted when encamp'd on Ilium's strand ;
Where throngs of brave souls from the light of day,
To the dim shades it hurried away (¹),
Leaving the bodies of those heroes slain
A prey to dogs and vultures on the plain—
(Yet was fulfilling, so, the will of Jove (²))—
From that sad hour when, first divided, strove
The king of men and Peleus' godlike son :
Say, then, of all the gods, who urged them on
In fierce debate, and hateful, to contend,
Turning their quarrel to that fatal end.
Latona's son, of whom great Jove was sire,
Kindled and fann'd in them the hostile fire ;
For to that god the king had given offence,
Therefore Apollo raised a pestilence

B

Among the ranks of the Achæan host,
That stood assembled on the Phrygian coast.
By that dire pest were heaps of warriors slain,
Because Atrides treated with disdain
Apollo's reverend priest, Chryses by name,
When to the swift ships of the Greeks he came,
And, as he paced along the adjacent shore,
The wreathed sceptre of his god he bore,
With a large ransom for his daughter fair,
The captive prize of Agamemnon there.
Suppliant he spake to all the Grecian host,
But to their leaders, the Atridæ, most:

    Ye sons of Atreus, and Greeks well greaved,
Pity the sorrows of a sire bereaved;
Then may the gods who on the Olympian hill
Their dwellings hold my fervent pray'r fulfil,
That Priam's city you may overthrow,
And to your homes with prosp'rous voyage go.
But now resign to me my daughter dear,
And take the precious ransom which I bear.
Thus acting, will you due reverence show
To Phœbus, god of the far-darting bow.

    The Grecians all, save Agamemnon, raised
A cheerful shout, and the proposal praised;
But he refused the parent's fond request,
And, him dismissing, these harsh words express'd.

    Take care, old man, that thee I find no more
Here at the hollow ships, or on the shore,
Now ling'ring, or, gone, return'd again
Thy suit to press, for thou wouldst plead in vain.

Even those ensigns of thy god display'd
Would prove to thee an ineffectual aid.
Thy lovely daughter I will not release
Till age fall on her and her charms efface,
Within my Argive palace, where she'll come
To dwell with me, far from her native home,
Tending my couch, and working at the loom :
This is my will, and such the maiden's doom.
Begone! I say; *vain's thy persuasive art :*
Provoke me not, that safer thou depart.

   Trembling, the old man fail'd not to obey :
Slow alongside the many-wavèd sea (³)
He silent moved; and then, apart retired,
By indignation mix'd with grief inspired,
To king Apollo, whom Latona bore
(That fair-hair'd mother), did he thus outpour
His pray'r :—O bearer of the silver bow,
Who around Chrysa thy defence dost throw,
And hallow'd Cilla, and dost bravely reign
O'er Tenedos, to hear me kindly deign.
Smintheus (⁴)! if e'er I did thy temple grace
With garlands fair, or on thine altars place
Of slaughter'd bulls and goats the fatted thighs (⁵),
Burning them down *to make an odour rise*
Grateful to thee, hear, and thy darts let fly
Among the Greeks, *whose king doth now defy*
Thy minister in me : Oh, make them pay
Dearly for all the tears I've shed this day!

   So spake he, praying : and the god, not slow
To hear and to avenge, with silver bow

And cover'd quiver on his shoulder hung,
Suspended by a belt around them slung,
Enraged at heart, from the Olympian height
Descending swift, came darkling like the night;
And, as he moved, impetuous and irate,
Rattled his winged instruments of fate.
When near the ships arrived, he sat apart;
And, having fitted to the string a dart,
He shot; and dreadful was the instant twang
Given by the silver bow, and far it rang.
'Gainst mules and dogs at first the arrows went,
Then 'mong the men themselves were thickly sent,
Making sad havock; and for nine whole days
Frequent and fierce the fun'ral fires did blaze
Throughout the camp; but, when the tenth appear'd,
Achilles' voice was in the council heard,
By him convened at the divine behest
Of white-arm'd Juno, who was sore distress'd,
Seeing such numbers of her Grecians slain,
And not in battle (⁶), on the hostile plain.

  The council thus convened, Achilles rose
His well-intention'd purpose to disclose.
Of all the chiefs the audience he claim'd,
But Atreus' son especially he named.

  Atrides (*so he call'd him*), we, I ween,
Would we ourselves from death inglorious screen,
Homeward must now return, since here to stay
Were to become to pestilence a prey.
But, I beseech you, let us now inquire
Of priest or prophet, whom the gods inspire,

Or dream-interpreter,—for Jove sends dreams,—
What this destructive visitation means.
The priest, or prophet, or interpreter,
Perchance may make the awful mystery clear
Why Phœbus nourishes such direful rage,
And tell us what his angor may assuage;
Whether he charges us with vows unpaid,
Or costly hecatombs too long delay'd;
Whether of perfect lambs and goats the steam
From burning altars rising he may deem
An off'ring meet; or yet what else may please
The god to accept, and thus his wrath appease.
　So spake Achilles, and thereon sat down:
Him follow'd Calchas, augur of renown,
Who things past, present, and eke future knew,
And pilot was of the whole fleet and crew
That came to Ilium; post to him assign'd,
Because, among th' endowments of his mind,
Was that prognosticating skill and art
Which it had pleased Apollo to impart.
　The augur then this prudent speech address'd,
Distinguishing Achilles from the rest.
Dear to the gods, Achilles, you require
Me to reveal the cause of Phœbus' ire;
Therefore I'll state it; but you first must swear
Both by your words and hands to keep me clear
From harm; for I expect the wrath to excite
Of a distinguish'd man, who rules with might
Among the Achæans, and whom all obey,
Without resistance to his wide-spread sway.

For a king angry has greater power
To injure than a man in station lower;
And, though his ire he stifle for a day,
It bides his time, and then will have its way.
So say, then, wilt thou me from danger save?
   Whereto Achilles him this answer gave:
Have perfect courage; fearlessly declare—
Whate'er thou know'st—the truth oracular;
For to thee, Calchas, solemnly I swear
By that Apollo who to Jove is dear,
And whose responses to thy pray'rs and vows
Thou to the Danaans truly dost disclose,
That while I live and see the light on earth,
No man, whate'er his station or his birth,
Shall at the hollow ships, or on the strand,
Against thee dare to raise a hostile hand;
And, though thou shouldst e'en Agamemnon name,
This promise shall remain in force the same.
   Being so assured, Calchas thus boldly spoke:—
That which Apollo's vengeance doth provoke
Concerns not vows, nor offerings delay'd,
But has regard to a fair captive maid (⁷),
Whom the king, Agamemnon, still detains,
While the prodigious ransom he disdains
Which her fond father, Chryses, at the fleet,
Suppliant and tearful, laid before his feet.
That rude refusal, ransom'd to release
The daughter, added to the foul disgrace
Heap'd on the reverend father, is the cause
Why the far-darting god his arrow draws:

For *that* he has inflicted all these woes,
Nor will he cease like evils to impose
Till, in obedience to the power divine,
The king the dark-eyed damsel shall resign,
Free and unransom'd, to her father dear,
And sacred hecatombs to Chrysa bear.
Then, and not sooner, we the god irate
Humbly may hope, calm'd, to propitiate.
    When thus the seer had spoken he sat down ;
And the wide-ruling king, with sombre frown,
Started, perturb'd, upon his feet,—his heart
With indignation fill'd, and poignant smart,—
His eyes all-flashing with a fiery light,
While, with a fierce distorted glance, their sight
Fell upon Calchas, whom he thus address'd :—
Prophet of evil ! ne'er hast thou express'd
Aught to me grateful ; but still to foretell
Impending ills to me doth please thee well.
Good hast thou never either said or done ;
And now among the Danaans me alone
Thou singlest out, as if to them I were
The cause of all this chastisement severe,
Because the splendid ransom I refused,
Of the priest's daughter, and him roughly used.
I will'd not it to accept in change for her,
Since her to Clytemnestra I prefer,
Whom, when a virgin, for my wife I led
(*Though never more, perhaps, I may share her bed*(⁸)),
While much I wish this maid to have at home,
When, there return'd, I shall have ceased to roam.

For not in form, or face, or gifts of mind,
By Clytemnestra is she left behind;
Nor in domestic duties is less skill'd:
Nevertheless, I am now prepared to yield,
Since it is best for all that I do so,
And thus preserve the people from more woe;
For I had rather they were saved than dead:
But you provide for me a meed instead
Of that whereof I'm presently bereft,
Lest I alone of all the Greeks be left
Without reward; for such a case all must
Pronounce to be unseemly and unjust.
Yet now my prize, ye all see, goes elsewhere;
Therefore, I say, a substitute prepare.

   Noble and swift Achilles answer'd then:
Most covetous and vain-glorious of men ([9])!
How can the magnanimous Greeks bestow
Such recompense as that thou'st named just now ?
No common treasures in reserve we own,
Since all the spoils of ev'ry captured town
Have been distributed; and to reclaim
And redistribute were both toil and shame.
But send the maid forthwith unto the god,
And if great Jove, who wields th' Olympian rod,
Shall ever on us the wish'd pow'r bestow
The Trojan well-wall'd city to o'erthrow,
Threefold and fourfold will we recompense
Thy present loss: *so now atone th' offence.*

   Then king Agamemnon in turn replied:
Godlike Achilles, do not thou abide

In the false notion, pow'rful though thou be,
That thou wilt circumvent or o'ercome me.
Is it thy wish thy own prize to retain,
When I shall have receivèd mine in vain ?
Dost thou require that I the maid restore ?
Then, if the Greeks her worth, . . . I ask no
Give in exchange, fitting the substitute [more, . . .
To my own taste, no longer I'll dispute :
But, if they will not give, myself will seize
Another's prize,—such as me best shall please ;
Be it Ajax's, Ulysses's, or thine,
And, having got it, lead it home as mine ;
While he whom I invade raves as he may :
But as to this, we'll treat another day.
At present let us from the laid-up fleet
Choose for our embassy a vessel meet,
In which, drawn down to the expansive sea,
Let oars and rowers well-appointed be ;
Next let the hecatomb be there convey'd ;
And, lastly, cause to embark the fair-cheek'd maid.
O'er all let a distinguish'd chief preside,
And for the conduct of the whole provide ;—
Ajax, Idomeneus, or Ulysses,
Or thy audacious self, Achilles !—
Who, by due rites done at the altar's pile,
The offended god to us may reconcile.

    This speech, so ended,—with an austere look
Achilles promptly show'd he did not brook ;
And, forthwith answering, to Atrides said,—
Oh ! fill'd with greed, with insolence array'd !

How, from this moment, canst thou once suppose
Any Achæan will in thee repose
His trust, obey thy mandates stern, or fight
Under thy banner,—thou who, proud, dost slight
Our counsel, and our service recompense
With high disdain, threats, and impertinence?
Me did no interested motive urge
Hither to come, braving the ocean's surge
With my good ships; nor had the Trojans given
To me offence, neither against me striven;
Ne'er did of boves or horses me despoil,
Nor waste the fruits of Phthia's fertile soil:
For shady mountains and resounding seas
Between my state and Troy their barriers raise:
But thee, man shameless, generously did we
Aid, that thy brother might avengèd be,
And thyself gratified with Trojan spoils,
Fruit of our valour and arduous toils;
For which no gratitude or care dost thou
By word or deed in any manner show;
Nay, even now, dost threaten to obtain
By force my prize, reward of toil and pain,
Which the brave sons of Greece were pleased to assign
To me; though never part equal to thine
Have I received, whene'er they've overthrown
And got the plunder of a Trojan town.
But, though my hands perform the greatest share
Of labour in this long and hapless war,
Yet, if to short cessation of our toil,
Perchance succeed division of the spoil,

By far the greater portion goes to thee,
While a small pittance only comes to me,
Who, withal grateful, to the ships retire,
Weary with fight, and spent with martial fire.
But home forthwith to Phthia now I go,
For this seems best; yet surely thou wilt know
Thy loss too late, because my pow'rful aid
By threats and foul dishonour has been paid.
When I'm departed I do not expect
That thou wilt long remain wealth to collect.

    To this Atrides, king of men, rejoin'd :—
Fly by all means, if so thy haughty mind
Thee prompt; not for my sake shall I essay
To keep thee here; others enough will stay
To reverence me; and, more than all beside,
Jove will me honour, and for me provide.
Of all god-nurtured kings thou art to me
The one most hateful; since most dear to thee
Are strife, dissension, and *wordy* war (¹⁰);
Concord and peace 'tis thy delight to mar.
If thou art mighty, this to a god thou ow'st,
And of the gift thou oughtest not to boast.
Now proceed homeward with thy ships and men,
And o'er thy Myrmidons in Phthia reign.
Thine ire I heed not, nor will I retard
Thy voyage; but, though thou may'st think it hard,
This threat I add :—Apollo having now
Deprived me of Chryseis, I will go
Myself into thy tent, and thence will take
Thy prize, Briseis, that, without mistake,

Thou, pow'rful as thou art, may'st surely know
I am, myself, more pow'rful than thou;
While others fear to claim equality,
Or make a bold comparison with me.

Achilles then, enraged and grieved at heart,
Was of two minds,—whether at once to start
With naked sword, and, thrusting quick away
Those who between them stood, Atrides slay,
Or calm his spirit and his rage control:
While thus distracted in his mind and soul (¹¹),
His sheath'd sword drawing, there was standing by
Pallas Athenè, sent down from on high
By Juno, who had equal love and care
For both:—Achilles, then, feeling his hair
Pull'd from behind, turn'd instantly his head,
And knew the goddess, who an aspect dread
Then show'd, designedly to him reveal'd,
While from the others she remain'd conceal'd.
Addressing her with wingèd words, inspired (¹²)
By wonder and surprise, he thus inquired:
Offspring of ægis-bearing Jove! why now
Art thou come here? .... to see and to allow
The injuries Atrides heaps on me?
Howe'er I'll speak out what I think will be
Accomplish'd soon;—that is, his life shall pay
For his mad pride and arrogance this day.

To whom Minerva, goddess azure-eyed,
In soothing accents thereupon replied:
By white-arm'd Juno I am sent to thee,
Thy wrath to calm, if thou'lt persuaded be.

You both are objects of her love and care;
Therefore of giving her offence beware,
And from contention cease, nor draw thy sword,
Though thou dost use many a railing word.
And thus I utter what the event will show,
That for the injury thou sufferest now
Thou shalt receive an ample recompense
In splendid gifts and acts of reverence:
Presents more costly thrice than thou'lt have lost,
With suppliant applications from the host.
But now forbear, and follow our behest :—
Then thus Achilles his assent express'd.

Me, goddess, it behoves your will to observe;
Nor, howe'er anger'd, shall I from it swerve.
'Tis best; for, whosoe'er the gods obeys,
Him chiefly they incline to when he prays.

He spake; and, yielding to divine command,
On the sword's silver hilt his heavy hand
He laid, and backward then into its sheath
Press'd down the glittering instrument of death,—
While she departed to th' Olympian height,
Where ægis-bearing Jove in mansions bright
Dwells ;—there with him and other gods to dwell,
Leaving Achilles his full mind to tell
To Atreus' son; for, though he had sheath'd his sword,
He spared no piercing glance, nor cutting word.

Drunkard ! with doglike eyes and deerlike heart,
Ne'er art thou ready from thy tent to start
With the arm'd phalanx of our host to fight,
Or on a place of ambush to alight

With the most valiant of the Achæan band,
For these are dangers which thou canst not stand.
Doubtless thou find'st it better far to stride
Throughout the Grecian ranks extended wide,
And bear away the valuables of those
Who dare thy greedy dictates to oppose.
Rapacious chief! people-devouring king!
Thou reign'st o'er worthless men, thus suffering
Such rule; else of thy wrongs, present and past,
What thou hast done this day would prove the last.
But hear what now I shall to thee declare,
And which, moreover, solemnly I swear,
By this my sceptre, which will never more
Produce green leaves, as wont in days of yore,
Ere in the mountains its trunk it left,
And by sharp iron was of bark bereft,
Which, thus transform'd, Achæan judges bear,
To whom's entrusted the defence and care
Of the just laws which were from Jove derived,
And through long ages have till now survived;—
This then's the mighty oath by which I swear:—
An hour will come of agony and fear,
When ardent longing for Achilles' aid
The breast of every Grecian shall pervade;
A time when thousands on the Trojan plain
Shall fall, by homicidal Hector slain;
Thyself, then sorrowing, wilt have no pow'r
To help or succour in that fatal hour.
Enraged and self-condemn'd, thou'lt feel the smart
Of thy injustice in thine inmost heart,

Because that in thy day of pow'r and pride
Thou didst dishonour, plunder, and deride
The best and bravest of the Achæan race,
And thereby bring upon thyself disgrace.

    Thus spake Achilles ; then upon the ground
He threw the sceptre, ornamented round
With golden studs, while he resumed his seat,
Atrides opposite, who raged with hate,
Yet spake not, check'd by Nestor, who then rose,
With the intent to calm those mutual foes :—
Smooth-speaking Nestor, Pylean orator,
A king revered, and prudent councillor,
From whose clear tongue, sweeter than honey, flow'd
A voice *where wisdom breathed, and feeling glow'd.*
So old was he that of " articulate men "
Two generations had pass'd since when
In Pylos he was born, and who of yore
With him had nurtured been—gone long before !
Over a third succession now he reign'd
In that famed isle, although at Troy detain'd,
Whither he came the Grecian cause to aid :
Addressing now the angry chiefs, he said,—

    Gods ! what distress and trouble will assail
The Achæan ranks, when they shall hear the tale
That discord fierce and deadly hate divide
Those who their battles lead and councils guide ;
While the report will pour an equal joy
Into all breasts within the walls of Troy ;
And, most of all, will the sad rumour's voice
Make Priam and his lusty sons rejoice.

But be persuaded now to cease from strife;
Ye both are young; heed one advanced in life:
For I was wont in by-gone years to hold
Counsel and intercourse with men more bold
Even than you; yet did those men of might
Never me contradict, or treat with slight.
Ne'er have I seen, nor ever yet shall see
Others of equal worth and bravery
To Perithous and Dryas, leaders famed,
Cæneus, Exadius, and divinely named
Polypheme, with great Theseus Ægides,
Resembling the immortal deities.
Bravest of all terrestrial men they were,
And of the strongest never had a fear.
Even the mountain-dwelling Centaurs they,
Daring to fight with, terribly did slay.
With them, however, was I in command,
From Pylos parted, far from Apian land,
Call'd by themselves away, for them to fight,
And fight I did according to my might.
But of all mortal men, such as men are
In this our generation, none would dare
Such fearful odds; yet those, being what they were,
My counsel willingly did ask and hear;
And when to them I had declared my mind,
To my persuasion they themselves resign'd.
Therefore do ye to my advice attend:
Now, and for ever, let your quarrels end.
And first, Atrides, let me thee advise
Not to deprive Achilles of his prize,

Which the Achæans previously gave,
But let him still retain his cherish'd slave.
And thou, Achilles shouldst submissive be
To him, who is superior to thee
As king,—ruling far more extensive realms,
And whose vast pow'r all others' overwhelms.
For surely other sceptred king ne'er gain'd
Such honour as Atrides has obtain'd
From favouring Jove; and, though thou stronger be,
That strength thy goddess-mother gave to thee.
So now, Atrides, suppress thou thine ire,
And thou, Achilles, quench thy angry fire;
For of the Achæans thou art the defence
And bulwark against hostile violence.

King Agamemnon then this answer made:
Doubtless, sage Nestor ([13]), what thou now hast said
Thy age and long experience well befits,
But this man no superior admits;
Rather he strives over all other men,
Including kings and chiefs, to rule and reign,
Expecting them his wishes to fulfil,
And all things ordering as suits his will;
Which I shall not permit, for this would be
Degrading to my rightful sov'reignty.
If the eternal gods him valour gave,
Does that entitle him to rail and rave,
And with contempt treat whom he should revere ? . . .

Achilles, interrupting, then and there
Replied: Timid and worthless certainly should I
Be thought and call'd, and that deservedly,

C

Did I in any way submit to thee :
Others thou mayst so rule, but never me.
Nor is it my intention to obey
Thy mandates more ; but one thing yet I say,
And to this, solemnly I charge thee, list :
The robbery of the girl I'll not resist ('⁴) ;—
Since what ye ᵃ had given me ye would now retract,
I'll not oppose so generous an act ;—
But of my other things in the black ship,
Take not thou, 'gainst my will, even a chip :
Try the experiment, that these may know . . . .
Soon thy dark blood around my spear would flow.
They having thus their angry words evolved,
Rose up, and the assembly was dissolved.
Achilles to the ships and to his tent,
Among his Myrmidons, with Patroclus went ;
The while Atrides caused a ship to glide
Down from the beach on to the flowing tide ;
For which he twenty skilful rowers chose,
With fitted oars ranging in equal rows :
Next for the anger'd god he caused to come
Into the ship the appointed hecatomb ;
Then, chiefly, leading her himself, he placed
The fair-cheek'd Chryseis, divinely graced.
Her follow'd the wise Ulysses, last,
Leader of all over the billowy waste.
Parted the ship, Atrides gave command
To purify the army on the strand.

ᵃ An apostrophe to the assembled chiefs, conveying a reproach for their tacit
acquiescence.

Lustration being finish'd, with due haste
The sordid wash into the sea was cast;
And, thus prepared, upon th' adjacent shore,
The god to appease, and pardon to implore,
A perfect hecatomb of bulls and goats
They sacrifice; while upward from it floats
A grateful scent that amicably blends
With curling smoke, and at Olympus ends.
    Meanwhile Atrides did not hesitate
The threaten'd injury to perpetrate:
Resolvèd still his object to obtain,
His active ministers and heralds twain,—
Eurybates and Talthybius named,—
He thus commission'd, with a soul inflamed.
Unto the tent of Peleus' son now go,
And thence, whether he consent or no,
Taking Briseis by the hand, her bring
To me, *her future lord, his present king.*
But if he shall the least resistance make,
I myself, thither going, will her take,
Assisted by attendants in such force
As shall for him render the action worse.
    Unwillingly the heralds bent their way
Towards the shore of the unfruitful sea.
When near the Myrmidonian ships they drew,
And the great chieftain's tent was full in view,
They him observed, sitting in silence there,
And halted with a reverential fear,
Showing reluctance in their looks; but he,
Though anger'd at their king's effrontery

(For well their hateful errand he divined
In his grieved heart and his foreboding mind),
Yet towards themselves he, seeing them distress'd,
Neither displeasure felt, nor ire express'd,
But bade them fearlessly approach his tent;
And from this speech they took encouragement.
 Welcome ! ye messengers of gods and men,—
For that ye are such do I clearly ken ;—
I blame not you, but him who sent you here
For fair Briseis, whom ye back may bear.
Noble Patroclus, go ; bring out the maid,
And give her to the heralds, who will lead
Her hence away to their despotic king;
But let them witness be of this one thing,
Before the blessed gods and mortal men,
With Agamemnon's self—harsh sovereign !
If e'er hereafter there be need of me,
From pest destructive other men to free. . . . .
 [*The speech thus broken may be understood
To indicate resolves of little good :—
Leaving that abjuration incomplete,
The following words he utter'd more sedate.*]
For surely fatal counsels sway his mind,
Unskill'd in present things, to future blind;
He cannot look behind him and before,
That so the brave Achæans, on the shore,
Or at the ships, for him might safely fight :
Such is his folly, such their wretched plight.
 He spake : Patroclus then, without delay,
Went, *little pleased,* his loved friend to obey;

And, having brought the damsel from the tent,
Consign'd her to the heralds; but she went
With them reluctant from the hero fleet,
Her destined lord, the tyrant king, to meet.

Then did Achilles on the tent-strewn shore,
Where the near sea a hoary surface wore (^{15}),
Looking beyond upon the purple deep,
Apart from his associates sit to weep;
And there, with arms outstretch'd and hands display'd,
To his fond mother fervently he pray'd.

Mother! he cried, since short-lived was the doom
Imposed upon me when I left thy womb,
Honour, at least, from Jove I ought to obtain
In recompense of so much toil and pain
As this short life brings with it; *while but few*
The pleasures are within my reach or view.
But honour'd me he has not in the least;
Rather, with his permission, I'm disgraced
By Atreus' son, who of the chief reward
Obtain'd by me in war, through conflict hard,
Deprives me now; *and I am left to grieve*
O'er contumely, with loss beyond retrieve.

Thus he spake weeping; and 'neath ocean's tide,
Where Thetis and Nereus in their cave reside,
She, goddess-mother, seated by her sire,
Hears her son's plaint, and favours his desire.
Emerged from ocean, like a vapoury cloud
Sailing through air, herself to him she show'd;
Then instantly before him sat, and tried
Him to console, while she her hand applied

To his wet cheeks, and stroked them as she spoke :
Tell me, she said, what griefs these tears provoke.

Achilles answer'd, with a deep-drawn sigh,
Thou know'st; why to thee, knowing all, should I
The events and circumstances now relate ?
Yet, since it is thy wish, I'll them repeat.
To sacred Thebes, Eëtion's seat, we came ;
And, having captured and sack'd the same,
We brought the spoils away ; of which, here laid,
Achaia's sons just distribution made.
For Atreus' son they fair Chryseis chose ;
Which choice hath proved the source of all our woes ;
For her sire, Chryses, reverend minister
Of king Apollo, came to ransom her ;
He for her liberation offering
A price immense to the proud Argive king.
But though the priest his sacred symbols bore,
And humbly king and people did implore,
While these the suppliant's request approved,
The monarch sat relentless and unmoved,—
Unmoved by pity, but stirr'd up to ire :
Sternly he bade the old man to retire,
Adding to the harsh command a threat
If he presumed his visit to repeat.

Aggrieved the father went, and sent a pray'r
To king Apollo, who his priest held dear ;
And, having heard it, granted the request,
Sending a deadly arrow—wingéd pest—
Swift through the Argive army, where they died
In heaps on heaps, as they fell side by side.

Then did a skilful seer, consulted, show
Wherefore Apollo drew his dreadful bow ;
Whereon I counsel gave that we should try
By proper means the god to pacify.
Then did king Agamemnon, from his seat
Rising, express a most offensive threat,
Which he has been not tardy to fulfil ;
For, when obedient to the sacred will,
He, though reluctant, yielded his consent
The maiden to release,—even while she went
In a swift ship by the Achæans mann'd
(Who with her bore to Chrysa's hallow'd strand
Gifts that were destined for th' offended god,
That he might turn from us the avenging rod),
Heralds arrived, by Agamemnon sent
Unto the hollow ships, and from my tent
Briseis took ;—her whom Achaia's sons
Had given to me, chief of the Myrmidons,
And her conducted to the tyrant king :—
Therefore do thou, seeing me suffering,
Assist me, since to assist thou hast the pow'r,
And give me solace in this evil hour.
Oft in my father's hall I've heard thee tell
How, when the other gods did once rebel,
By Juno, with Pallas and Neptune, led—
Conspiring to bind the Thunderer dread,
Thou only of the immortals didst him aid,
Calling Ægeon, who thy will obey'd
(Ægeon, whom the gods Briareus call),
Who, with his hundred hands, subdued them all ;

Then, placed beside heaven's liberated king,
He sat awhile joyful and glorying ([16]).
For his sire, Neptune, he in strength excell'd,
And with ease, therefore, the revolt he quell'd.
Him, thenceforth, did the rebel gods abhor,
And Jove to bind never attempted more.
This service, now, call to Jove's memory,
Embrace his knees, and beg his sympathy,
Beseeching him to espouse the Trojan cause,
Nor from the slaughter of the Argives pause,
Till at the ships, and even at the sea,
Driven and press'd, they there shut in may be,
That so they may their noble king enjoy,
Themselves being vanquish'd, and triumphant Troy ;
While Agamemnon, then, himself shall own
And feel his fault, in that the bravest son
Of the Achæans he dishonourèd,
And brought disgrace on his own haughty head.

    Him Thetis answer'd, shedding many a tear,
Why, O my son, did I thee fondly bear,
And bring thee forth, and thus far nurture thee,
The victim of an evil destiny ?
Would that thou mightest at the ships remain,
Tearless, and free from this thy mental pain ;
But since thou'rt both short-lived and desolate
Beyond all others, 'twas through adverse fate
I introduced thee to this hapless doom—
A life of sorrow, and an early tomb !
I will, however, to Olympus go,
Whose lofty peaks are all enwrapp'd in snow ;

With bland words thunder-loving Jove invade,
And use my utmost art him to persuade.
Meanwhile do thou to the swift ships retire,
And there against the Greeks nourish thine ire,
While thou from battle wholly shalt abstain,
And patient wait whate'er the gods ordain.
  Jupiter yesterday, having the intent
To grace the Æthiops' feast, to Ocean (^{17}) went
(A pious race are they): him follow'd all
The other gods—*a retinue not small.*
Eleven days there he purposed to remain,
And, on the twelfth, return to heaven again.
Forthwith thereafter to Jove's brazen hall
I'll go, and suppliant there before him fall,
Nor do I think my prayers will fruitless be.
Ended this speech she vanishèd; but he,
Whom in that place she left, there still remain'd,
Yet angry, and in mind most sorely pain'd,
Remembering the maid of beauteous zone,
Himself disgraced, and left to pine alone.
  Ulysses, now, to Chrysa having come,
In the good ship, bearing the hecatomb,
With Chryseis,—the crew, entering the bay,
The sails collected and them stow'd away ;
The mast, with all its tackling, next they lower'd,
And laid within its proper place on board.
The ship was then into the port profound
With oars propell'd ; next they the cordage bound,
And cast the anchors ; whereupon ashore
They went, and speedily the sacred store

For the god destined they there display'd;
Next, last, and best, debark'd the lovely maid.
Her wise Ulysses to the altar led,
Placed her within her father's arms, and said,—
Chryses, by Agamemnon I am sent,
Bringing thy child beloved, to the intent
That by her presence, and this offering
From the Danaans to thine incensed king,
They may his dreadful anger now appease,
And from his chastisement obtain release.
    With joy the father to his arms received
His late lost daughter, and no longer grieved.
    The Grecians now the splendid hecatomb
(Ready to undergo the sacred doom)
Around the well-built altar place; then take,—
Having first wash'd their hands,—the salt meal-cake.
Those rites perform'd, the priest, lifting his hands,
Before the altar, as he reverent stands,
With fervent accents offers up this pray'r :—
O Phœbus! who the silver bow dost bear,
Thou, who to Chrysa dost defence afford,
And art of Tenedos and Cilla lord
Supremely reigning,—thou, not long ago,
My pray'r for vengeance heard'st ; for mercy now
I beg; and as thou didst me honour then,
By punishing the Greeks, do thou again
Me honour now, by granting my request
That thou wilt instantly the plague arrest.
    Thus he spake, praying; and Apollo heard
With favouring ear the prayer so preferr'd.

Moreover, when they had pray'd and cast the meal,
The fatal strokes they to the victims deal.
First, drawing back the heads, they cut the throats,
And next strip off the shining hairy coats.
The sever'd thighs they cover with the caul,
After they'd doubled it, and had withal
Over the same raw morsels duly laid :
Then,—all these preparations being made,—
The fire was kindled with dry splinter'd wood ;
While round the pile the sacrificers stood,
And free libations pour'd of purple wine,
With invocations to the power divine.
The youths there present, holding five-prong'd spits,
Perform the function which them best befits.
The thighs being burnt, the men the entrails taste,
And into pieces small cut up the rest ;
Which being on those five-prong'd spits transfix'd
(Turn'd oft, and watch'd with care and skill well
They nicely roast, and, done, draw all away, [mix'd),
Thus finishing the labour of the day.
For the ensuing feast they then prepare,
Where all enjoy a full and equal share.
After their appetites were satisfied,
Boys, standing round, the bowls and cups supplied,
Which, crown'd with wine, were handed round to all ;
Then to the gods, upon whom they call,
Are due libations made, and through the day
They sing a propitiatory lay.
The Achæan youths a joyful pæan raise
To the far-darting god, whose loud-sung praise

Reaches his ear and gratifies his mind :
Thus pass'd the hours until the sun declined,
When evening shades dismiss'd to soothing sleep,
At the ship's cables, near the briny deep,
The wearied spirits of the festive crew,
Till rosy-fingered Aurora drew
Aside night's curtain ; then to th' army wide
Backward they sail'd over the ocean's tide.
Apollo granted them propitious gales,
That smooth'd their course, and fill'd th' expanded
On the erected mast ;—the purple wave   [sails
Roar'd round the keel, as it the surface clave,
And the ship glided swiftly on her way
Through foamy furrows and midst misty spray.
Having their voyage finish'd at the coast
On which encamp'd lay the vast Grecian host,
The black ship up they drew to the fast land,
And under-propp'd on the high bank of sand.
When this they had done, all th' assembled throng
Dispersed themselves the ships and tents among.
    Meanwhile Achilles, noble Peleus' son,
At the swift ships, discons'late and alone,
Sat nourishing his wrath, nor went again
Into the council of illustrious men,
Nor to the war ; though much he long'd to hear
The shout of battle, and the fight to share.
    While thus he sat, consuming his own heart,
Thetis was not forgetful of her part :
For, the appointed twelfth day having come,
The gods return'd to their Olympian home,

Jove going first, the others in his train;
She from her dwelling in the watery main
Early emerged, and to Olympus soar'd,
Where she found sitting heaven's sov'reign lord,
Loud-thund'ring Saturnian Jove, alone
And far retired, upon the highest cone ([18])
Of the celestial, many-peakèd hill,
Where he proclaims the dictates of his will.
There she before him kneels; upon his knees
Puts her left hand, and, while his face she sees,
She, with her right hand, takes his flowing beard,
In suppliant guise thus seeking to be heard.
   O father Jupiter! if ever I
Among the immortals did thee gratify,
Grant honour now to my sad short-lived son,
For the dishonour by Atrides done,
In having seized Achilles' cherish'd prize,
And boldly borne her off before his eyes.
For this dishonour from " the king of men "
Thee, both of kings and gods the sovereign,
Do I implore that thou, propitious, now
Wilt to my son redoubled honour show,
By granting to the Trojans victory,
Till by the Greeks he satisfied shall be,
With compensation for what he has lost,
And augmentation at still greater cost,
Adding to restitution of his own,
Increasèd honour for dishonour shown.
   Her cloud-compelling Jove no answer gave,
But musing sat long time, silent and grave;

While Thetis closely to his knees adhered,
And, urgent in her suit, thus persevered :
  Give me thy promise now, and by thy nod,
The solemn sign and sanction of the god,
Confirm it; or deny; that so I may
No longer at thy knees a suppliant stay;
Knowing myself assuredly to be
The goddess most of all contemn'd by thee.
Thou know'st no fear, *and whatsoe'er thou'st will'd,*
Thou lackest not the pow'r to see fulfill'd.
  Then cloud-collecting Jove to her replied,
While sore perplex'd, and heavily he sigh'd :
Surely a bad affair is this which thou
Wouldst now impel me to ; for well I know
The offence it will to haughty Juno give,
Who will her irritating taunts revive.
Ever among th' immortal gods does she
Rashly embrace each opportunity
To quarrel, while she asserts that I
Aid to the Trojans in the fight supply.
But now, lest jealous Juno should thee see,
Depart, leaving these things in care of me,
Who will perform—yet, come ; I will incline
My head to thee, making the solemn sign
Which 'mong th' immortals is the greatest known
To be vouchsafed on the celestial throne.
For what I promise, nodding with my head,
Can never be revoked, nor futile made.   [bow'd,
  After these words, heaven's king his forehead
And the ambrosial curls that clust'ring flow'd

Around his temples then were seen to shake,
Nor did Olympus' self avoid to quake ([19]).

    This matter settled, they separate went;
She to the sea making a swift descent;
Alert, and passing by a single bound
From bright Olympus to the gloom profound:
While Jove, in wonted dignity sedate,
With equal steps moved tow'rds his regal seat.
At his approach the other gods arose
From their respective stations of repose;
None on their seats presuming to await
His entrance, but all meeting him in state.

    So he resumed his seat upon his throne :
When Juno, cognizant of what he had done,
In furtherance of th' entreaty and design
Of silver-slipper'd Thetis, to repine
Ceased not; nor did she long delay to move
The dreadful anger of Saturnian Jove.

    Deceiver! said she, who 'mong the deities
Has counsel given thee ?—In colloquies
Sep'rate and secret 'tis thy delight
To form designs that may provoke my spite :
Nor ever canst thou bear to say a word
Freely to me, and of thine own accord,
Of aught that thou hast purposed to effect,
But leav'st me, when I am able, to detect.

    Her answer'd, then, of gods and men the sire :
Juno, I thee beseech not to inquire
Into my secret counsels, nor suppose
Thou art to know that which none other knows

Among th' immortals; difficult to thee,
Though thou my wife art, often would it be
To comprehend aright my deep-laid schemes;
Nor is the real always what it seems.
What it is right and fit for thee to know
None 'mong the gods or men sooner than thou
Shall be apprised of; seek to know no more:
In vain wouldst thou endeavour to explore
What I apart from the other gods decree—
Special prerogative of my sov'reignty.

   Prompt to the sov'reign ruler then replies
Venerable Juno of the ample eyes :—
Saturnius most severe! what sort of word
Hast thou this moment from thy lips outpour'd '
In no way ever have I heretofore
Aught of thee question'd, or sought to explore;
But vastly quiet, from intrusion free,
Thou plannest and perform'st what pleases thee :
Yet silver-footed Thetis, much I fear,
Hath with her silvery tongue beguiled thine ear;
For early this morning she sat by thee,
And suppliant placed her hand upon thy knee;
To whom I strongly do suspect thou didst
Promise her son to honour, and t' assist
The Trojans at the ships and on the coast,
By slaying many of the Grecian host.

   To this reply cloud-gathering Jove rejoin'd :
O sly one! ever thy suspicious mind
Thee urges into my affairs to pry,
And on my closest actions play the spy.

But, though my movements I may not conceal,
The knowledge of them will not prove thy weal;
Rather, the more distasteful to my mind
Wilt thou become, as thou wilt surely find;
And if, indeed, such the event shall be,
The greater pleasure it will yield to me.
Now silent sit, obedient to my word,
Lest all th' Olympian gods no help afford
To thee 'gainst me, if once my conqu'ring hands
I lay on thee transgressing my commands.

    He spake :—She, daunted by his words and look,
Her seat in silence and submission took,
Constraining her dear heart to bear its pain,
Since opposition appear'd worse than vain.

    The other gods who on Olympus dwell,
At this sad scene feeling their bosoms swell,
Express'd their grief in a united groan;
But Vulcan, artificer renown'd, alone
Ventured to make a speech; hoping thereby
Juno, his mother dear, to gratify.

    Her, with her husband-king, he thus address'd,
Speaking both for himself and for the rest :—

    Doubtless we here shall have a state of things
Intol'rable, if to these quarrellings
You two shall thus give scope, and thereby rouse
The other gods sides opposite t' espouse,—
All for the sake of men, *whose murd'rous strife*
Makes shorter still their natural span of life.
If discord 'mong th' immortals is to reign,
The hope of pleasant banquets will be vain.

My mother dear do I presume to advise,—
Though she is so intelligent and wise,—
To my dear father complaisance to show,
Nor more between them let dissension grow ;
Lest, if she do not her quick temper curb
The father should again our feasts disturb :
For if the Olympian Thunderer should choose
His pow'r and strength invincible to use,
He might us all from off our seats o'erthrow,
And hurl us to the farthest depths below :
But do thou now him with soft language soothe,
That he may show to us an aspect smooth.
    This having said, and risen from his place,
He, *with far more alacrity than grace,*—
Being lame,—a double wine-cup to her bore,
And in bland words addressèd her once more :
Bear and forbear, my mother, though thou be
So sad ; lest I should be obliged to see
Thee, whom I love so much, in far worse plight,
By being beaten and chastised outright,
When I should not be able to afford
Protection or defence by deed or word :
For hard to deal with is th' Olympian king
By other gods,—doing or suffering,
When their desires with his designs conflict,
In aught he may command or interdict.
This my own sad experience has taught ;
For once, when 'gainst him I would help, he caught
Me pow'rless by the foot, and forthwith hurl'd
Over heaven's threshold to the nether world.

During the day continued my descent ([20]),
And, with the *sun's*, I reach'd *my* occident,
With little life left in me when I fell
In Lemnos, where the shepherds used me well.

    At this last speech white-armèd Juno laugh'd,
And readily the nectar-cup she quaff'd,
Then to the other gods he nectar pour'd
From a capacious beaker on the board.
At view of Vulcan thus minist'ring
Did th' Olympian halls with laughter ring
Among the blessed gods, who all the day
Kept up the banquet; nor in any way
Was there aught wanting to produce content:
The muses, all, their genial influence lent;
And with Apollo's lyre in concord sweet,
Alternate voices made the quire complete.
But when the western sun's declining light
Was follow'd by the soothing shades of night,
The immortals to their sep'rate halls retired ([21]),
For Vulcan's architecture much admired.
Th' Olympian Thunderer, then, the stately bed,
Where he accustom'd was to lay his head,
Ascended; and, reclined, *a short time* slept ([22]);
And Juno, near him laid, *no vigil kept.*

Book II

THE other gods and heroes slept all night ;
From Jove alone refreshing sleep took flight.
He was debating in his anxious mind
By what expedient he the way should find
For Thetis' son due honour to procure,
And the Achæans to destruction lure.
This, then, at last, the best to him did seem—
To send to Atreus' son a treach'rous dream.
    These winged words, therefore, to it he spake :
To Agamemnon's tent, ere he awake,
Go, fatal Dream, and instantly relate
To him all that I now to thee dictate.
Command him to arm the Grecian bands
In all their force ; for that into his hands
Instantly shall fall the wide-streeted town
Which yet the Trojans proudly call their own ;
Since Juno now has to her will inclined
Those gods who erst were of a different mind.
    When thus heaven's sov'reign had express'd his
The Dream made haste the mandate to fulfil :   [will

Sudden and swift towards the ships it went,
And there proceeded to Atrides' tent.
Arrived, it found him in a sleep profound,
And, standing near his head, where thought was
Assumed the Nestorian form, and seem'd [drown'd,
Nestor himself, whom the king much esteem'd.
In this guise, therefore, did the Dream divine (¹)
The royal sleeper's passive mind incline.

 Sleepest thou, son of Atreus, sage and brave?
It ill becomes a man of counsel grave,
The guardian of his people, whose welfare
Should be the object of his watchful care,
To sleep all night : now, then, give heed to me,
Who am the messenger of Jove to thee ;
For, though thou art from him at distance far,
That distance does not thee at all debar
Of his protection, nor yet make him less
Compassionate towards thee in thy distress.
For thine own interest, hither to thy tent
Me, with instructions urgent, he hath sent,
Commanding thee to arm the Grecian bands
In all their force ; for that into thine hands
Instantly shall fall the wide-streeted town
Which yet the Trojans proudly call their own ;
Since Juno now has to her will inclined
Those gods who erst were of a different mind.
Remember this :—let not oblivion take
The place of slumber, when thou shalt awake.

 Its function ended so, the false Dream fled,
Leaving the cheated sleeper in his bed,

On things fix'd not to be to calculate
As upon things already fix'd by fate.
For confident he felt that very day
In Priam's captured town he should display
His conqu'ring banner, and reap the spoils,
For rich reward of his protracted toils.
Far was the thought from his deluded mind
What griefs and troubles lay conceal'd behind
The flatt'ring picture which the Dream had drawn,
What ills would follow the next morning's dawn;
The bloody battles which had been decreed
By Jove, in long perspective to succeed
Between the Grecian and the Trojan bands
Ere Troy should fall into the Grecians' hands,
When these at last full dearly should have paid
For the dishonour on Achilles laid,—
Thousands on thousands suffering for one,—
That one himself, who had the injury done!
　　Roused up from sleep while yet he seem'd to hear
The voice divine in Nestor's accents clear,
Upright he sat; then a soft tunic new
Put on, and o'er it a large mantle threw;
On his smooth feet he beauteous sandals tied;
Suspended from his shoulder, at his side,
He girded on his silver-hilted sword;
And lastly—that which chiefly he adored—
His sceptre ancestral he took, and bore
As forth he issued to the neighb'ring shore,
Where the Achæan ships lay idly moor'd,
While they the baffled enterprise endured.

And now Aurora to Olympus soar'd,
Where radiant light she on th' immortals pour'd.
Meanwhile the king to his loud heralds gave
Orders to summon to a full conclave
The long-hair'd, brazen-mailed Achæan bands,
There to deliberate, and receive commands.
Those, having their due ministry perform'd,
These to the council sedulously swarm'd ;
But th' Argive king had prudently thought fit
A senate first at Nestor's ship should sit.
When the assembled leaders had appear'd,
His object he thus openly declared.

Hear me, my friends ! A dream divine by night
Came to me—visible to mental sight,
And no less audible to the lull'd ear
Than would a palpable form appear
And speak to one who, being wide awake,
Of all he saw and heard should knowledge take.
In form, and stature, and corporeal mien,
As Nestor's self that dream by me was seen ;
And then it spoke in tones of Nestor's tongue,
These words divine, which in mine ears were rung,
As the form venerable stood o'er my head,
While I in dulcet sleep lay on my bed.

Sleepest thou, son of Atreus, sage and brave ?
It ill becomes a man of counsel grave,
The guardian of his people, whose welfare
Should be the object of his watchful care,
To sleep all night : now, then, give heed to me,
Who am the messenger of Jove to thee ;

For, though thou art from him at distance far,
That distance does not thee at all debar
Of his protection, nor yet make him less
Compassionate towards thee in thy distress.
For thine own interest, hither to thy tent
Me, with instructions urgent, he hath sent,
Commanding thee to arm the Grecian bands
In all their force; for that into thine hands
Instantly shall fall the wide-streeted town
Which yet the Trojans proudly call their own;
Since Juno now has to her will inclined
Those gods who erst were of a different mind.
This counsel bear in mind. Thus the Dream spoke,
And disapppear'd : then I from sleep awoke.
But now be active ; and for the fight
The forces arm, according to our might.
In the first place will I myself essay
Their courage,—bidding them to flee away
In the swift ships ; then you, to counteract
That counsel, shall employ your skill and tact.
    Then Nestor sage, of sandy Pylos king,
Foe both to flattery and to bickering,
But now deceivèd by the Jove-deceived,
In the speech following his mind relieved.
    Friends, princes, and leaders of th' Achæan host,
Had any other man ventured to boast
Of revelation such as that declared
By Agamemnon, which ye now have heard
From his own lips, and doubtless truly told,
I should have thought the tale a falsehood bold,

Or else the dream itself a thing of nought,
Which therefore merited no serious thought.
But HE, supreme of all the chiefs and kings
Whom this disastrous war to Ilium brings,
Hath seen the vision, and heard its voice :—
Therefore it seems to me we have no choice
But well, and quickly as we can, to arm
Achaia's valiant sons without alarm.

When thus he had spoken he prepared to quit
The court ; nor did the rest there longer sit.
The sceptre-bearing kings all followèd
That shepherd of the people, as he led.

Meanwhile the common people throng'd to know
What their great leaders should resolve to do :
And, as the busy bees in vernal hours
Fly here and there, hov'ring about the flow'rs,
Issuing in clusters from the hollow rock,
Awhile dispersing, but again to flock
Together ; ever their collected store
Of sweets into the common hive to pour ;
So do the Greeks from every ship and tent
Where lie dispersed th' inactive armament,
Proceed in ranks along the wide-stretch'd strand,
Or, congregate, in frequent groups they band.
Among them Fame, the messenger of Jove,
Ardent, impels them onward still to move
To the great meeting ; promptly they obey'd,
And the earth groan'd beneath their heavy tread
While there they met and sat ; and all around
Tumultous voices made the place resound,

Until nine heralds in their midst arose,
And bade the throng their spirits to compose,
That they might hear what those would have to say,—
Jove-nurtured kings,—who over them bore sway.
    Scarcely had ceased that loud plebeian din,
When Agamemnon's royal form was seen
~~To rise,~~ holding the sceptre which, by Vulcan wrought,
The artist-god a gift to Jove had brought,
Which Jupiter gave next to Mercury,
Who with the same did Pelops gratify ;
Pelops, in turn, not long time afterward,
On Atreus, people's shepherd, it conferr'd.
This symbol—powerless in a monarch's grave—
Atreus, dying, to Thyestes gave ;—
Thyestes, rich in flocks and herds, who then
Gave it to Agamemnon, king of men,
That over Argos and the isles he might
Therewith dominion exercise, and right.
Upon this sceptre leaning, thus he spoke :
    In my perplexity I you convoke.
Hard is my fate, since Jove has me deceived ;
For he once promised me—and I believed—
That strong-wall'd Ilium I should overcome,
And have a prosperous voyage home.
That promise, now, by fraud he nullifies,
After the direful loss and sacrifice
Which we've endured in the delusive hope
Nought could th' eternal ruler's word revoke.
But now me, reft of honour, he constrains
To quit this scene of fruitless toil and pains,

And home to Argos sail, worse than I came—
Then strong, now weak; then honour'd, now in shame.
Such is the will of him who has o'erthrown
The stately towers of many a prosp'rous town,
And many more will doubtless overthrow,
Resistless both to raise and to lay low.
Shameful 'twill be for after-times to hear
The sad recitals of this hapless war ;
How the Achæans, num'rous and great,
Could bear such ignominious defeat ;
Since such it must appear, if 'twas in vain
We fought (though not yet vanquish'd) on the plain,
Warring 'gainst men comparatively few ;
For, if the Greeks and Trojans a review
Of their respective forces wish'd to take,
And for that purpose they a truce should make,—
Each being number'd (the Trojans all
Comprising such as citizens they call),
And should th' Achæans into tens divide,
While, that their tens might be with wine supplied,
Each decade must a single Trojan take,
Of him their wonted cup-bearer to make,
Many a decade would remain in need :
So much our aggregate does theirs exceed.
But num'rous auxiliaries the Trojans have,
From other cities brought,—men strong and brave,
Who still prevent me wishing to destroy
The well-inhabited streets of Troy.
Nine years at length have come and pass'd away,
While our good ships were falling to decay,

Their timbers rotting, and their tackling loose,
The natural effects of long disuse :
Meanwhile, at home, our little ones and wives
Wait our return (*if happily our lives*
Be spared) *to gladden them and us at last,*
When the war's toils and perils all are past ;
Not thinking that the work for which we came
Is unaccomplish'd, *like an empty dream.*
Since such the case is, act as I advise ;
Abandoning the luckless enterprise,
Let us depart from this detested shore,
And see our own beloved land once more.
Not yet shall we Troy, " city of broad ways,"
Capture : so will we brook no more delays.

 This speech fail'd not the minds to agitate
Of those—the most—who could not penetrate
The counsels of the senatorial band,
Who o'er the multitude possess'd command.

 Such tumult then did the assembly show
As when, at once, the south and east winds blow
From out the clouds of Jove, raising the waves
Of the Icarian sea, and tempest raves ;
Or as a gale that, rushing from the west,
Sweeps o'er expansive corn-fields, late at rest,
Bending the slender stalks with well-charged ears,
So the commotion in that throng appears.

 As, shouting, to the ships in haste they went,
Their rapid feet thick clouds of dust up sent.
Mutual exhortations then were heard
To seize the ships,—to have their grooves well clear'd,

And, next, from beach to sea to draw them down;
While all are stirr'd by thoughts of home alone;
And, as their hands this labour occupies,
Redoubled shouts of "home!" ascend the skies.

Then surely, spite of fate, they had return'd,
Had not queen Juno, who the case discern'd,
Her counsel with Minerva thus renew'd :—

Daughter of Jove! and ever unsubdued,
Shall thus the Argives o'er the watery main,
By shameful flight their native land regain,
And,—boast of Priam and the Trojans,—leave
Her for whose sake at first they cross'd the wave ?—
Argive Helen—her whom to obtain
So many thousands on the hostile plain
Have perish'd, far from their loved fatherland ?
But do thou hasten to the Achæan band,
And, by the strength of thy persuasion mild,
Deter them from a course so base and wild;
Nor suffer them to launch upon the deep
Their ships :—these must their wonted station keep.

So Juno spoke; and Pallas azure-eyed
On the Olympian height did not abide
An instant ere she the command obey'd,
But rapidly,—soon as the words were said,—
She downward flew, and at th' Achæan fleet
Ulysses found—that chieftain most discreet,
Whom one with sov'reign Jove might well compare
For skill in counsel, but whom now despair
Seem'd to subdue : standing he was apart
From the black ship, while sorrow fill'd his heart.

Him in this state approaching, Pallas said :
  Son of Laërtes ! man of prudent head
And valiant heart, thus is it that ye flee
To your loved homes and country o'er the sea,
Which bore you hither that you might regain
Argive Helen, for whom you will in vain
Have fought, and many thousands lost,
Leaving her here a glory and a boast
To Priam and the Trojans ?—But go now
To th' Achæan people ; to them show
The folly and disgrace of such a flight,—
As thou canst do in its most proper light ;
Using persuasive words and accents bland,
More pow'rful oft than harsh and stern command.
Nor cease from thy persuasion till thou'st gain'd
Thy point, in having every one restrain'd.
  She spake : he heard her ; nor did he delay,
But running at full speed, he threw away
His cloak, which Ithacan Eurybates,
His herald, pick'd up, while as yet he sees
The chief before upon his mission bent ;
The herald follow'd him as on he went,
Until by Agamemnon he was met,
From whom he then,—more influence to get,—
Received the sceptre of Atrides' line,
That incorruptible gift divine.
Arm'd with this awful instrument of might,
He rush'd among the ships prepared for flight.
And whomsoever he there met or found,—
Man of no note at all, or man renown'd,—

Him he address'd according to his grade;
And thus to men of rank and pow'r he said:
  Most reverend sir! assuredly 'twere wrong
In you, to whom true valour should belong,
To act a dastardly or trait'rous part;
Go, brave yourself, and use your utmost art
Others to turn from this their base design,
Nor let them for their homes untimely pine.
Sit you yourself, and make the others sit,
Until the council shall have judged what's fit.
As yet you are ignorant of Atrides' mind;
The Greeks he now is trying; and they'll find
That punishment will follow them who thwart
His plans and purposes, by force or art.
Not all have heard what he in council said;
Caution must then be used, lest, angerèd,
He on th' Achæans some evil bring,
For great's the wrath of the Jove-nurtured king.
Honour proceeds from Jove, and him Jove loves;
Therefore to honour him it all behoves.
But whatsoever common man he saw,
Or, shouting met, to him he show'd no law,
But with the royal sceptre gave a stroke,
While in the manner following he spoke:—
  Sirrah! sit down; the words of others hear,
Who thy superiors and betters are;
Neither in battle, nor in council, thou
Didst any merit in thyself e'er show.
By no means here can we men all be kings;
Nor is it in the scheme of social things

A good when many the dominion share;
The rule of one man better is by far.
One prince alone, that monarch let us have,
To whom the wily son of Saturn gave
The sceptre, and the laws by which to reign :—
Thus did Ulysses his part well sustain,
The host controling, who from ev'ry side
Where spread the camp and navy far and wide,
Hasten'd again into the council's pale,
With din tumultuous—such as doth assail
The adjacent continent, when billows roar
On the deep sea, and beat against the shore.
    Seated at length the throng, the tumult dies,
When in their midst a form is seen to rise,—
A man with convex back and concave breast,
And with a tapering head, which has for crest
A single lock of thinly-growing hair,
Leaving elsewhere the vertex wholly bare.
He squinted too, and of one foot was lame.
Such was his form; Thersites was his name.
And the distortions of his perverse mind
With its odd framework aptly were combined.
In language scurrilous he was profuse;
His chief delight the princes to abuse;
But lower game he oft would not disdain,
If any how a laugh he could obtain.
Of all the men whom Greece to Ilium sent,
He might be term'd the foulest miscreant.
Achilles and Ulysses had been they
Against whom oftenest he would inveigh,

Hating them most of all : but since 'twas known
The Greeks had with Atrides angry grown,
That king himself he ventured to deride,
And in shrill accents now to him he cried :
   Wherefore complain'st thou? what is now thy need?
Thy tents are full of wealth, which might thy greed
Suffice to appease; and thou hast also there
Numerous women, both select and fair,
Whom we have given to thee, who first of all
Art served, whene'er into our hands there fall
The spoils of conquer'd towns; yet still more gold
Desirest thou?—a son's rich ransom told
Into thy coffers, by his father found,—
Some wealthy Trojan,—whose son, being bound,
Is led by me, or by some other Greek ?
Or dost thou now another damsel seek,
With whom to indulge in amorous delight,
Sharing thy board by day, thy couch by night ?
Never, by any means, ought prince or king
To bring upon his people suffering.
Enough that one Chryseis, for thee gain'd,
Caused us a plague, being by thee detain'd.
Oh, base, weak, cowardly, ignoble race !
No longer Greeks, ye who your sires disgrace ;
Why do we not with our swift ships depart,
And leave him here to cultivate the art
Of cooking wealth himself, without the aid
Of those whose service he has ill repaid ?
That so he may by his experience know
Whether we are to him a help or no,—

E

Who even now affects with contumely
Achilles braver man by far than he;
Whom he has robb'd of his most valued prize,
Whereby both law and honour he defies.
But in Achilles' heart exists no gall,
Else surely, son of Atreus, of all
The injuries thou hast or wilt have done,
The last were that to Peleus' noble son.
   So railing at royal Agamemnon,
Thersites spoke; and, instantly thereon,
Noble Ulysses, roused, against him stood,
And, frowning, thus indulged his angry mood.
   Thersites! most incontinent of speech,—
Fluent in base revilings!—cease to screech;
Nor wish to be thyself the only one
Who acts irreverently towards the throne.
Thee do I reckon the most troublsome
And vile of men that have to Ilium come
As followers of Atrides; wherefore now
No more, with unclean tongue and shameless brow,
Cast foul reproaches upon honour'd kings:
In all 'tis wrong—most wrong in underlings.
Nor does it thee, or such as thee, become
To fix the period for returning home.
We know not yet what turn these things may take,
Nor whether of our fortunes now at stake
Adverse or prosp'rous will be the event,
While of the homeward voyage, consequent
Upon that issue, we know not the fate,—
If it be well, or ill, or soon, or late.

Thou bidest there, hurling thy censures vile
'Gainst Agamemnon, because erewhile
The Danaan heroes with munificence,
His various toils and cares did recompense.
But I declare to thee, if e'er again
I catch thee in the like abusive strain,
No more Ulysses' head thenceforth shall rest
Upon his shoulders, nor he stand confess'd
The father of Telemachus, if then
I do not strip thee in the sight of men,
And, having beaten thee from head to hips,
From the place drive thee blubbering to the ships.

  So spake Ulysses; and, as this he said,
On the reviler's back a blow he laid,
The sceptre using, which thus caused to rise
A bloody tumour; while forth from his eyes
He pour'd a flood of tears; and, as they flow,
He writhes his shoulders, smarting from the blow;
Then down he sat, afflicted with disgrace,
And wiped the tears from his begrimèd face.

  The rest, though sad themselves, at this sight
And for a moment their own cares beguiled, [smiled,
As one man, looking to his neighbour said,
Of all the good deeds that are justly laid
To great Ulysses, this by far's the best
That he has stopp'd the abuse and set at rest
The tongue of that rude slanderer; who no more
For certain will his objurgations pour
On kings; nor yet his counsels more obtrude:
Such was th' opinion of the multitude.

Then the great chief (still sceptred) rose again,
His views and feelings, this time, to explain.
There stood before him, in a herald's guise,
Enjoining silence, the goddess wise,
Blue-eyed Minerva; giving this command,
That all might hear the speech, and understand.
Attention thus secured, the chief began
His well-considered speech; and thus it ran :—
Alas ! a most opprobrious disgrace
In the esteem of the whole human race
The Greeks would lay, Atrides, upon thee,
Were they now home from Ilium to flee ;
Breaking the solemn promise to thee made
When Greece they left the Trojan realm to invade ;
That sacred promise Troy to take or burn
Ere to their fatherland they would return.
But lo ! forsooth, resembling tender boys,
Or widow'd wives, whom thought of home employs,
Those men who were so valiant erewhile
Are now effeminate and puerile.
And, truly, I confess 'tis very hard
For disappointed men to be debarr'd
From all the sweets of a beloved home,
Confined to foreign shores, or forced to roam.
The sailor, only one short month detain'd
By wintry winds and storms, sits inly pain'd
Beside his ship, viewing the surge and spray,
And thinking on his wife, so far away.
For us, not one short month, but nine long years,
With all their toils and troubles, hopes and fears,

Have borne us downward on the stream of time
Since, confident, we left our native clime,
With all our lovèd ones, and hither came :
Therefore by no means I th' Achæans blame
For their impatience at the curved ships,
Since the disasters which our hopes eclipse :
Still 'tis an evil *hard to be sustain'd,*
With shameful loss, without our object gain'd,
To reimbark the remnant of that host
And quit discomfited the hostile coast,
Leaving old Priam to enjoy his state
In the proud domes we came to devastate,—
Leaving fair Helen to her Trojan lord,
Instead of having her to him restored,
Her rightful lord, on whose account alone
We came—all we had hoped for left undone !
Endure awhile, my friends, until we see
The truth or falsehood of the prophecy
That Calchas utter'd, which I still retain
In mind, and all can witness who remain
Spared by the fates—how erstwhile when the fleet
Of the Achæans did at Aulis meet
To bear destruction to the walls of Troy,
And we were occupied in the employ
Of offering to th' immortals sacrifice,
Near to the fountain where the altars rise,
Under a beauteous plane-tree, whence a stream
Of limpid water flows with silvery gleam,
A sign portentous came upon our sight,
By Jove himself protruded on the light ;

For, gliding forth beneath the altar's foot,
A dreadful serpent to the plantain's root
Slid,—his bright back with crimson spots bespread;
And when he there arrived, raising his head
Up to the branches which afforded rest
Within their foliage for a sparrow's nest,
Eight youngling birds there, first, he made a prey;
And as the parent-bird in misery
Scream'd, and around the nest kept hovering,
The ruthless serpent seized her by the wing;
Then, having her within his coils o'erpow'r'd,
Ending her agony, he her devour'd.
Another wonder thereupon was shown;
For lo! the serpent was turn'd into stone;
Being thus transform'd by cunning Saturn's son,
To the amazement of the lookers-on.
Those portents following the hecatomb
Calchas pronounced were signs of Ilium's doom;
And thus the revelation he made clear:—
Why, said he, Grecians, stand ye mute with fear?
Provident Jupiter this wond'rous sign
Exhibits to us as a work divine;
Late, of late issue, but of lasting fame,
Which it to future ages shall proclaim.
Eight years, therefore, let it be understood,
Are represented by the youngling brood;
The mother, then, the ninth year indicates,
Which we must war before the Trojan gates;
And, in the tenth, on the ensanguined plain,
Troy and fair Helen we shall have for gain.

So spake the prophet, and the event is near ;
For now have we commenced the final year.
Wait calmly, then, ye well-arm'd Grecians all,
Till Ilium's ramparts shall before you fall ;
And then, in spoils and honours, you'll obtain
Full compensation for your hard campaign.

When this judicious speech had reach'd its close,
Loud acclamations from the crowd arose,
Echo'd among the ships and 'long the shore,
Where the Achæans, changed in mind, no more
Press'd for departure ; but now all combined
To praise the utterance of that godlike mind.

Among them, next, Gerenian Nestor stood,
And from his lips pour'd this impetuous flood :

Good gods ! he cried, ye men act more like boys
That have not yet quitted their childish toys,
And much less practised the art of war,
Though ye have toil'd and travell'd long and far.

Whither, I pray you, are about to pass
Your oaths and compacts ?   Like to wither'd grass
Kindled by fire, will they all end in smoke,
And nought but animosity provoke ?
The counsels and the cares of worthy men,
Such as the Argives were esteemèd then,
In vain we seek for ; or, if them we find,
They are unheeded as the passing wind ;
And should these wranglings e'er so long extend,
They'll not conduce to any useful end.
But, Agamemnon, be of constant mind,
As heretofore, and let no counsels blind

Divert thy purpose; but command the host
In arduous battles; nor count the cost
Of two or three dissentients, who apart
Conspire that we for Argos should depart
Before we know whether correct will prove,
Or false, the promise of shield-bearing Jove :
But their conspiracies will not succeed ;
For I'm assured 'twas otherwise decreed
By the supreme Saturnian Jove, that day,
When we from Greece for Ilium sail'd away
In the swift ships, threat'ning the Trojan race
With slaughter, desolation, and disgrace ;
As then the Thunderer on the right hand peal'd—
An omen which success to us reveal'd.
Wherefore let no Greek thought of home accept,
Till with a Trojan wife he shall have slept.
But should the heart of any Grecian burn
With the desire of earlier return,
Let him his hand upon his black ship lay,
That, before others, he may die that day.
But thee, O king, I reverently advise,
Thyself well couns'ling, neither to despise
Another's counsel, nor at once refuse
This, which I think thou prudently may'st use.
The men by districts and by tribes arrange,
That these, being not to one another strange,
May mutual assistance easier lend,
To attack the foe, and from attack defend.
By such arrangement, too, if all agree,
The faults and merits we at once may see

Of ev'ry leader then, and private man,
And be enabled, on the slightest scan,
The coward to distinguish from the brave ;
Thereby, moreover, shalt thou knowledge have,
In case the issue be unfortunate,
On whom, or what, to charge our adverse fate ;—
Whether to the opposition of the gods
(*Case tantamount to overwhelming odds*),
Or our own warriors' cowardice and sloth,
Or ignorance of the art of war, or both.

 To him responding, Agamemnon said :
O venerable sage ! would that I had
Among the sons of the Achæans here
Ten others such as might with thee compare
(For thou in counsel dost surpass us all) ;
Then would king Priam's city quickly fall
Into our conqu'ring hands, with all its spoil :
But Jove surrounds me with a fatal coil,
Me dooming to a state of ceaseless strife,
And fierce contention that embitters life.
From this fatality my quarrel rose
With swift Achilles, for no other cause
Than this—that I a girl took from his tent,
Of which, as the aggressor, I repent.
But were that luckless breach between us heal'd,
The present gloomy cloud would be dispell'd,
And the misfortunes which us now annoy
Would thenceforth fall upon devoted Troy.
Now, without more debate, go, all, and dine,
Then, fortified within by food and wine,

Let every man his outward arms prepare,
And ready make for th' impetuous war,
By his spear whetting, bracing on his shield,
Feeding his horse well for the battle-field,
Viewing his chariot on ev'ry side;
And let no other cares the day divide,
Which must be giv'n entirely to fight,
Without an interval from morn till night.
The thong of every buckler then shall sweat,
And ev'ry bosom where a heart shall beat;
And every hand that lance or spear doth grasp
Must ache, while he who wields the same will gasp
For breath, from hurling it without a pause;
And ev'ry horse shall pant that chariot draws.
But whomsoever lingering behind,
Or lagging at the curved ships I find,—
Assuredly that coward's flesh and blood
For dogs and vultures shall be drink and food.

Ended this speech, the Argives shouted loud,
As when the south wind urges ocean's flood
'Gainst a projecting rock on some high shore,
Where the rough billows never cease to roar,
Nor ever leave the promontory dry,
Whatever winds exert their agency.

Up starting,—towards the ships the people haste,
And in the tents dispersed take their repast,
Having first kindled culinary fires,
From which the smoke ascends in frequent spires.
There each man doth his proper god implore
For his protection in the coming hour,

Hoping therefrom that in th' impending strife
The god propitious will preserve his life.

The king of men to Jove, the supreme king
Of all the gods, meanwhile an offering
Prepared—a fatted ox, five years of age,
And the chief men invited, prince and sage,
To the ensuing feast; among whom were,
With Nestor and Idomeneus, that pair
Of noble heroes, the Ajaxes named,
Tydides brave, and great Ulysses, famed
For excellence in counsel, oft compared
To Jove himself: moreover there appear'd
King Menelaus, who, *far from the least,*
Was welcome, though an uninvited guest.
He knew his brother had no slight design'd,
And what anxieties disturb'd his mind.

About the ox they stood, all in a ring,
Raising the meal, while fervent pray'd the king:

Most glorious, great, and cloud-compelling Jove,
The blest ethereal mansions far above
Inhabiting enthroned, let not the light
Of setting Phœbus leave earth veil'd in night,
Ere I king Priam's palace overthrow,
And, with his gates, wrap it in fiery glow;
Nor till, well hack'd, the corslet I shall tear
From Hector's valiant breast, and make him share,
With many of his friends, a dusty bed,
From which he never more shall raise his head.

Thus Agamemnon pray'd, but the great god
Did not vouchsafe the ratifying nod,—

Though he the sacrifice did not disdain,—
While he intended far more toil and pain
For the Achæan host ere their distress
Should terminate in vict'ry and success.

However, when they had pray'd, and cast the meal,
The victim's head back forcing, with the steel
They cut his throat, next skinn'd him, then the thighs
Sever'd, and cover'd with the caul in plies,
Involving with the same crude morsels strew'd;
All which they burnèd down with dry cleft wood.
The entrails, fix'd on spits, next they suspend
Over the embers, and duly tend.
The thighs being burnt, the entrails next they taste;
The rest in slices cut on spits are placed,
And duly roasted; then all drawn away;
When,—thus their duty done,—without delay
The men prepare the feast, and fairly share
Their proper portions of the abundant fare.
When so the appetite of every man
Was sated, the Gerenian chief began:—

Most excellent Atrides, king of men,
Thee will I venture to advise again.
That we no longer precious time may waste,
The work deferring which great Jove has placed
Into our hands, let heralds cause to meet
All the confed'rate Grecians at the fleet,
While we, the assembled chiefs, proceed to inspect
The array, and all that's needful to direct;
Stirring the multitude to use their might,
Nor lose their courage in the coming fight.

So Nestor spake, and promptly such command
Atrides gave his heralds close at hand :
They proclamation made accordingly,
With which the people hasten'd to comply.
　　Then Agamemnon and the other kings
Themselves arranged the more important things,
Assigning to each tribe throughout the host
(*As Nestor had advised*) its proper post.
While in the midst Minerva azure-eyed
Bore, buckled to her arm close to her side,
That precious ægis, proof against decay,
On which a hundred fringes, hung, display
Their texture of pure gold that splendid shone,
Of which the sterling worth of every one
Equals a hundred beeves ; and, with this shield,
She ranges o'er the plain—soon battle-field—
Among th' Achæan ranks, who quickly feel,
Urged and inspired by her, the strength of steel ;
And martial ardour kindles in each breast,
With thoughts of home no longer now opprest :
Rather does war to them more sweet become
Than lately was the thought of going home.
　　As when consuming fire some forest vast
Upon a mountain's top, its gleam doth cast
O'er th' adjacent campaign far and wide,
So does the splendour of their armour glide
Through the clear air, as it to heav'n ascends,
While o'er the plain their rapid march extends.
　　And, as the many tribes of feather'd race,　[geese—
That haunt the streams and pools—cranes, swans, and

In meads of Asius, about Cayster's banks,
Variously must'ring in flocks or ranks,
Hither and thither hov'ring on the wing,
Exultant, as they cackle, scream, or sing,
And as their groups successively descend
Into the vale, a clang they upward send,   .
In numbers such, from ships and tents pour'd forth,
Over Scamander's plain, shaking the earth,
With echoes to the din of men and steeds,
All hasten to perform heroic deeds.
And numerous as are the leaves and flow'rs
That spring upon the lap of nature pours,
So infinite on Scamander's spacious plain
Those warriors stand, preparing all to gain
The promised victory, by vain hopes cheer'd :—
Moreover, as when oft in spring, his herd
Milking, the rustic swain fills his clean pail,
Thick swarm the flies that swain and herd assail,
Buzzing and hov'ring constantly around,
So swarm on the intended battle-ground
The Greeks innumerable in armour bright
And crests high-waving, thirsting for the fight.
    As shepherds easily can separate   .
Their flocks and herds, however congregate
They mix and wander o'er the pasture-land,
So of the army, those who had command,
According to their tribes and companies,
Marshall'd them all distinctly, and with ease,
In military order ere they went
To battle : among whom pre-eminent

Was Agamemnon ; both in eyes and head
Like thund'ring Jove, fit for inspiring dread;
In waist like Mars, like Neptune in the breast,
As strength and bearing are thereby express'd.

And, as the bull, surpassing all the herd,
Is seen conspicuous, so then appear'd
King Agamemnon beside the rest,—
Chieftains and kings—the greatest and the best.
Thus Jove ordain'd he should on that day seem,
That all should reverence his sway supreme.

Teach me, ye Muses, who celestial seats
Inhabit, and from them beheld the feats
That day perform'd, or present at them were
(While only vague reports have reach'd our ear),
The chiefs and princes all of Greece to name;
For of the host at large to extend the fame
Were task too hard for one of mortal mould,
Since . . . that their exploits bold might all be told . . .
Ten mouths, ten tongues, a voice that cannot break,
Would not suffice; and, could they duly speak,
Still would be wanting a brazen heart,
The needful strength and ardour to impart,
Unless the heavenly Muses, daughters fair
Of ægis-bearing Jove, the work should share,
Relating all, and who to Ilium came:
Leaders and fleets, then, only will I name.

Peneleus and Leïtus the Bœotians led,
Who, partners in command these others had;—
Arcesilaus and Prothoenor,
With Clonius also, their coadjutor.

Them follow'd the dwellers on the rocks
Of Aulis,‸with all those hardy stocks
Who Hyria, Schœnus, Scolus, Eteon
(The hilly call'd) inhabit,—towns well known;
With Thespia, Græa, and the plains
Of Mycalessus (*city that retains*
The name which it derivèd from the cow (²)
That there to Cadmus famed of old did low,
When he was searching for the destined site
Of future Thebes, guiding his footsteps right);
They whom Harma and Ilesius own'd,
Erythræ too, and whom Eleon found,
Peteon and Hyle, Ocalea, Medeon
(This being by repute a well-built town);
Copæ, Eutresis, and, famed for doves,
Thisbe; they who possess'd, fitted for boves,
Haliartus, "the grassy" rightly named,
With Coronēa, for its grain well famed;
They who in Glissa and Platæa lived,
And they too who in Hypothebæ thrived.
Onchestus next, that mighty Neptune own'd
For tutelary god, and hence renown'd,
Being withal a highly beauteous place,
Whose solemn groves no impious footsteps pace;
Arnè abounding in fruitful vines,
On which the sun with rip'ning radiance shines;
Nissa, city eminently divine,
With which Medēa willingly we join;
And, last, Anthēdon, Bœotia's extreme,
Find 'mong their warriors, all and each, a name.

Fifty good ships made up Bœotia's fleet,
In ev'ry one of which were seen to meet
Of her brave sons thrice forty fully told,
Making six thousand in the whole enroll'd.

Ascalaphus and Ialmenus renown'd,
Who fair Antioche for mother own'd
(A virgin pure until by Mars deflour'd,
In Actor's hall surprised and overpow'r'd),
Led forth Orchomĕnos and Asplēdon's host
Confed'rate, which of thirty ships could boast.

The brave Phocenians to the fight were led
By Schedius and Epistrophus, both bred
By great Iphitus, hero of renown,
Their sire, who Naubŏlus for his did own.
Issued from Cyparissus, and the rocks
Of Python (*destitute of herds and flocks*),
Crissa divine, Daulis, Panopea,
High-raised Hyampolis (³), and Anemorea,
Added to those who nigh the noble stream
Cephissus named (*whose sacred waters gleam
Through rich Bœotia in their beauteous course*)
Were wont to dwell; and where that river's source
Is found,—Lilæa, fountain of fair fame :
This race in forty ships together came.
Arrived, on the Bœotians' left hand,
Arming in due array, they take their stand.

Oïlean Ajax swift, led to the field
The Locrian force : he was of smaller build
And shorter height than Ajax Telamon,
But still with him could bear comparison

F

For bravery and skill in arms; while he
Unequall'd stood for his dexterity
And force in hurling the tremendous spear,
Stranger alike to rashness and to fear.
A linen corslet on his breast he wore
When he himself into the battle bore.
The Locrian army by this Ajax led
Comprised such men as had inhabited
Cynus, Scarpha, Opoeïs, and Bessa,
Thronius, Augæa fair, and Tarpha,
With those who dwelt about Boagrius,
And such as issued from Calliarus.
Those, Locrians all, were from beyond the bound
Of rich Eubœa, and their force was found
Contain'd in forty vessels, which had brought
Them safe to Troy, where finally they fought.
　　The valiant Abantes then follow'd :—
Those who Eubœa had inhabited;
They who from Chalcis and Eretria came,
And Histiæa of distinguish'd fame
For the abundance of its purple vines;
Those from Cerinthus on the sea's confines;
And those from Dios next, a lofty town
With citadel and battlements that frown;
They whom Carystus own'd; and those who came
From Styra :—of this force the leader's name
Elphēnor was,—a branch of mighty Mars,—
Son of Chalchōdon, and enured to wars.
Him follow'd the Abantes, swift as wind,
Having bare foreheads, and long locks behind;

Skill'd in the use of the projected spear,
And eager all to prove it in the war,
Splitting therewith the hauberks of the foes
Who in th' approaching fight should them oppose.
They, with himself, in forty vessels sail'd
Nor on the Trojan coast to land had fail'd.

Athens well built, most celebrated town,
Whose people for their king of yore did own
Erectheus (*and were therefore often named*
The Erecthidæ) sent her sons much famed.
Erectheus was the progeny of Earth,
Whom she produced by an unwonted birth;
But Pallas rear'd him, and her temple made
His home; and there by sacrifices laid
Upon her altar (⁴) the Athenians show
The gratitude which they the goddess owe
For the protection which their state obtains;
Whence she the name Pallas Athenè gains.
Over the Athenian army held command
Menestheus, to whom no man in the land
Was equal in arranging for the war
Both men and horses, and the warrior's car,
Nestor alone excepted, for the age
And longer experience of that sage.
In fifty black-prow'd ships from Attic land
Th' Athenians had been borne to Ilium's strand.

Huge Telamon twelve ships led, which contain'd
All of the men from Salamis obtain'd;
And these he placed beside the Athenian host:
Next following them those from the Argive coast,

And they from well-fortified Tyrintha,
Hermiŏnè and Asĭnè with deep bay;
Trazēnè, Eïon, Epidaurus set
With vines; and those Achæan youths whom late
Sea-girt Ægina, and Masēta held:
These Diomed, who much in arms excell'd,
Join'd with Sthenĕlus (the beloved son
Of Capaneus, prince renown'd) led on.
With these joint leaders went, over that band,
Godlike Euryălus, third in command
(The son he was of Mecisteus, whose sire
Was Thaläus, a chief of martial fire);
But Diomed was o'er them all supreme;
And fourscore ships transported him and them.
    Mycenæ, populous and magnificent,
And Corinth, elegant and opulent,
Well-built Cleōne and, next, Orneia,
Serene and pleasant Aræthyria,
Sicyon, where at the first Adrastus reign'd,
And the repute of a good king maintain'd (⁵);
High Gonóëssa, Hyperesia,
Pellēnè, Ægium, and Helicè,
Together with the towns throughout the coast,
Supplied Agamemnon's proper host,
Which did a hundred complete ships demand
For their conveyance to the destined strand.
His forces better and more num'rous were
Than those of any other leader there.
In burnish'd armour he himself array'd,
And gloried in the excellence display'd

In his own person and his proper band,
As on he moved and exercised command.
  With Menelaus sixty vessels came,
And the brave crews who mann'd and fill'd the same
Were all by those localities supplied
The names whereof shall now be specified.
First of the number Lacedemon's glen;
Pharè and Sparta next, and Messa, then,
Made vocal by the frequent ring-dove's moan,
Helos, a town maritime well known;
Amycla, Brysia, and Augēa fair,
With the two towns that severally bear
The names of Laas and of Œtўlus :—
But Menelaus brave, impetuous,
His own host (ranged apart) in grief address'd,
Exhorting them, in his private interest,
To avenge the outrage of Helen's case,
By ruin to the Trojan realm and race.
  Next are the sources of Nestor's aid,
Which ninety ships to Ilium had convey'd.
Arenè fair, Æpy well-built, and Pylus,
With Thryum by the fords of Alpheus;
Cyparissa with its gloomy shades;
Amphigenēa with its fertile meads;
And Pteleos, and Helos, and Dorion;
Which last, *if fame can be relied upon,*
Is the place where the Threïcian poet met
From the offended Nine his cruel fate.
For Thamyris, vain man! did rashly dare
Himself with them in talent to compare ·

And he had even ventured to pretend
In the melodious art them to transcend.
Challenged they vanquish'd him, then struck him
And of the tuneful gift deprived his mind.   [blind,
　Royal Agapenor, who did next succeed,
Supplied such force as threescore ships to need
For transport; but all those ships were found
By Agamemnon,—Agapenor's ground
Being all inland; and therefore he
Had neither ships, nor knowledge of the sea;
But his brave troops in feats of arms were skill'd,
And these the races which their phalanx fill'd.
Those of Arcadia's sons who at the base
Of Mount Cyllēne dwelt, a warlike race,
Accustomed to combat hand to hand;
The men of Pheneus, a gallant band;
Those of Orchomenus (in whose rich meads
Many a flock of sheep, with cattle, feeds);
Ripè and Stratia also; with whom were
Those of Enispè bleak,—Mantinea fair;
Stymphalus and Parrhasia, and the youth
Of Tegea, *brave, if history speaks truth* (⁵).
　Of Elis, a populous and fertile seat,
Buprasium, abounding much in wheat,
And all that district of land that's seen
Myrsinus and Hyrmin's towns between,
Th' Olenean rock, and the Alysian fount,
The leaders and their ships assembled count
Four of the first, and forty of the last,—
Ten to each chief, whose force, singly not vast,

Combined to make a powerful complement,
Who, all Epēans, in those vessels went.
Amphimachus and Thalpius the leaders were
Of two divisions, having each a share;
Of whom the one was son of Cteatus,
The other being son of Eurȳtus,
While both descendants of Actor were;
But of the other two, who likewise there
Command of the Epeans held, the one
Diores was, of Amarynceus son,
Polyxenes the other,—form divine,
A chief renown'd and of th' Augēan line—
Son of Agasthĕnes, Augeia's son,
Augeia, who had sat on Elis throne.
　　Those of Dulichium, and the sacred isles
Which look o'er sea to where fair Elis smiles,
Call'd he Echinădes, Meges, the son
Of Phyleus dear to Jove, and whom perhaps none
Excell'd in arms ("equal to Mars" 'twas said)
Obey'd as chief, and follow'd where he led.
Phyleus, his sire, anger'd, had in past time
Renounced his father's house, and native clime;
And, having wander'd long, at length had come,
Tired, to Dulichium, his future home;
And there did Meges, Phyleus' son, obtain
Twice twenty ships that sail'd with him and train.
　　Next by Ulysses of resplendent fame
Were led the forces which united came
From Ithaca, from Neritus wood-crown'd,
And fertile Cephallenia sea-bound;

With them who had dwelt in Crocylia,
And those whose homes were rude Ægilipa ;
Those whom Zacynthus and Samos own'd,
And those who dwellings in Epirus found.
With them who came from th' Ionian strand;
The whole of whom, placed under the command
Of their great chieftain, freely with him went
In twelve ships red-prow'd to Troy's continent.
   Thoas, illustrious Andræmon's son,
Who ruled the Ætolian realm alone
(Since Meleager, and the other sons
Of Œneus, the sov'reign who ruled it once,
Had died), commanded all the men who came
To Ilium under th' Ætolian name,
Including, severally, those whose own
Abodes were Olenus, fair Calydon,
Pleuro, Pylēne, Chalcis on the coast :
Those, all forming the Ætolian host,
With that brave leader full well content,
In forty vessels to Ilium went.
   Idomeneus, spearman of illustrious fame,
The Cretans ruled ; among whom they name
Gortȳna, Cnossus, *cities both which own'd*
Warriors, as skilful bowmen, far renown'd ;
Lyctus, Lycastus white, and Rhytium,
Miletus and Phæstus ; which make the sum
Of forces Cretans named : but, beside these,
Were many other troops that cross'd the seas
With brave Idomeneus ; for widespread Crete
A hundred cities had, whose aggregate

Found men enough quite fourscore ships to fill,
And who, therein embark'd, obey'd his will;
Though he was assisted in command
By fierce Meriones, on sea and land;—
Meriones,—warrior so bold and fear'd,
That like the god of war he oft appear'd.
    Tlepomenus, warrior tall and brave,
Nine ships conducted o'er th' Ægean wave,
Mann'd by proud Rhodians, parted into three
Tribes, which dwelt sep'rate, though join'd at sea.
Camirus, Lindus, and Ialyssus claim'd
As theirs the honour of these Rhodians famed;
And the illustrious leader of all these
Astyocheia bore to Hercules,
When her, become the partner of his bed,
From Ephyre and Selle's banks he had led,
Resting awhile after he had display'd
Heroic feats, and towns in ashes laid.
Tlepomenus, distinguish'd among all
As dext'rous spearman in his father's hall,
Had scarcely attain'd to manhood's prime,
When he Lycimnius, hoary grown by time,—
His father's uncle,—lucklessly there slew,
And therefore from his native land withdrew.
By his race threaten'd, with ships he fled,
And numerous adherents with him led.
Many and hard afflictions he endured,
Ere finally safe refuge he secured:
But this at generous Rhodes at length he found,
Where his three sep'rate bands he spread around;

And, in the love of Jove supremely blest,
Enjoy'd, with them, great riches, peace, and rest.
  Nereus, whom to Charŏpus Aglæa bore,
Three ships from Syma to Ilium's shore
Led forth; the fairest he in form and face
(Except Achilles) of the Grecian race,
Among all those who had arrived at Troy;
But he the character did not enjoy
Of a courageous warrior; and few
The foll'wers were whom in those ships he drew.
  Nisȳrus, Casus, Crapathus, and Cos (⁷),
City where ruled Eurypylus,—with those
Islands Calydnæ named, their troops sent forth,
Under two leaders of valiant worth,—
Brothers,—Antiphus and Phidippus named,
Whose sire, a son of Hercules most famed,
Was Thessalus call'd: nor did they fail
To Ilium with thirty ships to sail.
  Now must the faithful muse at length record
Whence came the warriors brave, whom, as their
In fifty ships Achilles led to Troy,   [lord,
But, there arrived, their force delay'd to employ,
Since at the fleet the godlike hero lay
(Disgusted with the king) for many a day;
Angry and sad for fair Brïseis' sake,
Whose loss had caused his vengeance to awake.
Her as his own he had gain'd among the spoils
Of Thebes and of Lyrnessus after toils
Num'rous and hard, wherein he had o'erthrown
Epistrophus and Mynes of renown,

W̶h̶e̶ sons w̶e̶r̶e̶ of Selepiades[b] the king :
But though his wrath so long lay smouldering
Against Atrides and his friends, he rose
At length, and turn'd it on his country's foes.
These are the countries and towns which sent
Under Achilles, their large armament :
Pelasgian Argos, Phthia (*where was born*
The hero,—and where—he gone—lived forlorn
Peleus, his aged sire, hoping in vain
After Troy's fall to see his son again) ;
Trechina, Alos, Alŏpe ; and, for dames
Beauteous famed, Hellas :—under which names
Myrmidons, Hellēnes, Achæans—*all*
Prompt to obey their mighty leader's call,
Soon ás his anger should cease to burn
Against Atrides, and on Hector turn.

  Phylăce and the flow'ry Pyrrhăsus,
Land dear to Ceres, as fructiferous,
Iton, productive of fleecy flocks,
Antrona maritime, with caves and rocks,
And Pteleon that in fertile meadows thrived,
Their forces sent, and they at Troy arrived
In forty ships, by Protesilaus led,—
The first to land there, first there to lie dead :
Leaping ashore, a fated Dardan dart
Met his bold advent, and pierced his heart.
In Phylăce he left a loving spouse
To tear her cheeks, and an unfinish'd house.
But his brave band were not left destitute
Of a commander skill'd and resolute.

b A patronymic of Evēnus.

Their new chief was the brother, not so old
As Protesilaus, nor perhaps so bold :
Podarces was his name ; the sire of each
Iphiclus, son of Phylacus, man rich
In flocks and herds : the brothers were esteem'd
Much by their troops, and heroes rightly deem'd.
But though the forces faithfully adhered
To the surviving brother, they revered
And cherish'd with regret and fondness most
The dead, who had been their glory and their boast.

 From Pheræ, and Bœbe, where expands
The lake Bœbean call'd, their martial bands,
With those by Glaphÿræ and Iölcos sent,
Led by Eumēlus, in eleven ships went.
Son of Admetus, by Alcestis, he ;
Of all the Pelean daughters loveliest she.

 Methone, Melibœa, and Thaumasia,
With rocky Olïzon upon the sea,
All their assembled force together brought,
Their ships being seven ; and each of them was
With forty rowers, skilful bowmen all ; [fraught
Of Philoctētes they obey'd the call ;
But this brave leader, bitten by a snake,
Languid and sick at Lemnos, they could take
With them no farther ; and him, suffering there,
They left, though him to leave they sorry were.
Arrived at Ilium, soon they call'd to mind
Their dear commander who remain'd behind.
In the mean time they wanted not a chief,
Medeon, as such, coming to their relief

(Whom Rhena illicitly to Oileus bore),
And them he led to the appointed shore.

From Tricca, and Ithome mountainous,
Where glens and lofty crags are numerous,
And from Œchalia, town of Eurytus,
Issued those led by Podalirius
And by Machāon, leeches both renown'd,
Who Æsculapius for their father own'd.
Th' assembled forces by those brothers led
Were o'er the sea in thirty ships convey'd.

Those whom Eurypўlus, Evēmon's son,
Illustrious, in forty ships led on,
Were from Ormĕnium, and from the sides
Of the Hyperian fount, whose water glides
In crystal streams; together with the band
From Titan's chalky height, and from Asteria's land.

White Oloösson, Orthe, and Gyrtonè,
Together with Argissa and Elōnè,
Sent forth their troops led by that valorous
Chief Polypœtes; he whom Perithöus
(Whose parentage t' immortal Jove is laid)
For son by fair Hippodamia had,
On the same day when he the shaggy race
Of Centaurs punish'd and put in chase.
Having slain some, he then from Pelion's height
Pursued to Æthicæ the others' flight.
But not alone did Polypœtes guide
The last named forces; since they at his side
Leonteus had, a dauntless branch of Mars;
And those two jointly led them to the wars

In forty ships.—Leonteus, be it told,
Was from Corōnus sprung, a warrior bold,
Who from one Ceneus had his birth derived;
And with the son's, the father's name survived.
    From Cyphus, by Guneus at their head,
Were safely two-and-twenty vessels sped,
With the Enienes, the Peræbi bold,
And those who dwelt about Dodona cold;
With those who occupied the pleasant meads
Where Titaresius in meanders leads
His gentle stream, which into Peneus glides,
Though they together never mix their tides.
The placid Titaresius, smooth as oil,
Careless of silver-eddying Peneus' toil,
Flows ever undisturb'd upon the face,
Being of inviolable Stygian race.
    Swift leader Prothöus, of Tethrēdon son,
Those who round Peneus dwelt, and Peleon,—
Peleon the grove-crown'd,—brave Magnesians they—
In forty ships transported o'er the sea.
These were the last of all the Grecian train
That cross'd, for Ilium bound, the watery main.
    Say next, O Muse, who 'mong the armament
Of the Atridæ were most eminent
In worth,—excelling in heroic deeds,
And who among them had the noblest steeds.
Of mares the noblest were of all by far
Those of Eumēlus, a most well-match'd pair,
Being the same in colour, height, and age,
As eagles swift, and full of martial rage:

On the Pierian hills, by Phœbus bred,
To battle they were eager to be led.
Of heroes Ajax Telamon was best,
While for a time Achilles was at rest,—
At rest his body—restless in his mind;
Nor could the whole Achæan army find
Achilles' equal, nor steeds match for his:
But, now secluded, his sole thought was this—
To be revenged, and wait the promised day
When Agamemnon for his wrongs should pay.
His soldiers meanwhile on the tented ground,
Near to the sea, in exercises found
Amusement in lieu of war's exploits—
Hurling the spear, with archery, and quoits.
The steeds unharness'd, at each chariot's side,
With lotus green and parsley wild supplied,
Regale themselves; while all the chariots stand
In order due according to command,
Beneath the shelter of the canvas shades;
The charioteers, as each his fancy leads,
Roaming about the camp in anxious care
For their great leader now inactive there.
   (⁸) *Except those Myrmidons, thus separate*
By the command of their great chief irate,
The host were moving as if all around
The plain were scorch'd, while the disturbèd ground
Groan'd, as when lightnings of angry Jove,
Descending from the surcharged clouds above,
On Arima (⁹), the place where it is said,
Huge Typhon in his mountain bed is laid,

Assault with vengeance the enormous tomb,
While hollow bellowings issue from its womb.
 Now, with a message charged of grave import,
Did Iris, swift as wind, to Troy resort,
Despatch'd by Jove; and there, at Priam's gate,
Where he with old and young in council sate,
Met them, assuming both the form and voice
Of Priam's son, Polites, who, by choice
Confiding in his speed, himself had placed
Upon the tomb of Æsyētes, raised
High-tow'ring o'er the wide-extended plain,
To observe the coming foe;—and she began :—
 My aged sire ! talk ever doth thee please,
And now art thou discoursing at thine ease,
As if, forsooth, this were a time of peace;
Yet, though I've seen much war, such an increase
Of warriors as advancing now appear,
Thick as the leaves or sands, still drawing near,
Ne'er have I seen before; and all around
The town they throng, to make its walls our bound.
But, Hector, thee I strongly recommend
To this my counsel promptly to attend,—
That, since within the boundaries of Troy,
Many auxiliaries we now employ,
The tongues they speak being various as the men,
Their leaders so shall marshall them, that when
For battle they are met, each shall command
His own compatriots, who will understand
His orders, and disorder thus avoid,
While they by no discordance are annoy'd.

Thus Iris spake; nor was great Hector slow
To approve the counsel, and obedience show.
Forthwith the mix'd assembly he dissolved,
And in immediate action was involved.
To his behest obedient all, to arms
They rush'd, changing debate for war's alarms :
The gates of the vast city open flew,
And 'midst a deaf'ning din they pourèd through,
Into the spacious plain, a train immense
Of warriors, horse and foot, for Troy's defence.
Before the town, apart on level ground,
Lifts its high head a most distinguish'd mound
Of earth, by men Batiæa named,
But as Myrinna's tomb—amazon famed—
By the immortal deities esteem'd :
There the surrounding territory teem'd
With Trojans and their allies ranged for war,
And these their forces in particular.

Great Hector, fierce and ready for the fight,
In his own person led the Trojan might,
Including the most valiant of the host,
As well as of its numbers, too, the most.

Æneas led the Dardanians forth :
Of Venus by Anchïses was his birth,
In Ida's dells(¹⁰), the fruit of fond embrace
Between the race divine and human race.
But not alone he led the Dardan band,
Since with him were, associates in command,
Archilochus and Acămus, whose sire
Antenor was, man famed for val'rous fire.

G

The rich Zeleians, Trojan race, who drink
At Ida's foot, clear waters on the brink
Of the Æsēpus, follow'd to the fight
Lycaon's son, brave Pandărus, who might
And skill possess'd to use the precious bow
Which on him erst Apollo did bestow.
　　They whom Adraste and Apæsus own'd,
Tereia steep, and Pityeia (crown'd
With pines), thence led, form'd a united band
To combat under the combined command
Of Amphius and Adrastus : their sire
Was famed Percosian Merops, whose desire
It was, knowing their fate, them to prevent
From joining the Trojan armament.
And he, unrivall'd seer, to them foretold
The consequence of such their conduct bold ;
But they regarded not the prophecy—
Impell'd to choose their course by destiny.
　　Of them who in Arisba dwelt, and Sestus,
Percōte, Practius, and Abydus,
Himself, as head and only leader, sees
(And rightly placed) Asius Hyrtacides,
Renown'd for dauntless courage, and whose steeds
Were such as suited his heroic deeds :
Splendid, and of superior birth, they bore
Him from Arisba, and Selleis' shore.
　　The spear-arm'd Pelasgians, wont to toil
Upon Larissa's deep and fertile soil,
Hippothöus led forth, but not alone ;
Pylæus, who of the same sire was son,

Commanded with him ; and they owed their birth
To Lethus,—sire conspicuous for worth.
  Acămas and Pirüs, of the Thracians
Led those whom surgy Hellespont contains.
  Euphemus, of Trœzēnus (Cëӱ̈ѕ' son)
The son, led the Ciconians alone.
  The warriors of Pæonia, who had come
From distant Amȳdon, their native home,
Where Axius broad and ever beauteous flows ([11]),
Men valiant and dext'rous at their bows,
Pyræchmes for their only leader own'd :
  While them from Enĕtum, for mules renown'd,—
Them from Cytōrus, for its box-wood known,—
From Sesămus, a lofty sea-coast town,—
From splendid habitations on the sides
Of the Parthenian stream (*that northward glides,*
And falls at length into the Euxine deep),—
Them from the heights of Erythīnus steep,—
From Cromna, and the rude Ægialus,
Pylæmenes, a chief conspicuous,
This Paphlagonian force to Ilium brought,
And with them on the side of Priam fought.
  From distant Alybè, in whose rich mines,
Conceal'd, the silver metal grows and shines,
The Halizonians march'd ; and at their head
Epistrophus and Odius, who them led.
  Over the Mysians Chromis did preside,
With Ennomus, the augur, at his side ;
But not by auguries could he dark death
Escape : in Xanthus' stream he fell beneath

The stroke of swift Eacides, with more
By many who had fought upon that shore.
  Phorcys, and godlike Ascanius, the band
Of Phrygians led from far Ascania's land;
All of them glowing with a strong desire
In battle to employ their ardent fire.
  Mesthles and Antiphus two brothers were;—
Pylæmenes their sire;—them to him bare
Gygæa, who was then Nymph of the lake
When he was wont there his abode to make
At Tmolus' foot: and now they, men full grown,
Led the Mœonians to Troy's doomèd town.
  Marshall'd by Nastes and Amphimachus (¹²),
The sons of Nomion, men illustrious,
Came from Miletus, Phthiræ crown'd with woods,
Mycale's summits, and Mæander's floods,
The Carians, people of barb'rous tongue,
Accordant with the source from which they sprung.
But vain Amphimachus, foolish as bold,
To battle went bedeck'd, girl-like, with gold,
Gold which, alas! from death could not redeem:
Under Achilles' sword, sunk in the stream,
He lost his life; and then the glitt'ring spoil
Served to reward the fierce conqu'ror's toil.
  The men from distant Lycia, on the banks
Of eddying Xanthus, constitute the ranks
Which ranged in order under the command
Of blameless Glaucus and Sarpedon stand.
  *And these brave warriors complete the list
Of forces met the Grecians to resist.*

NOTES TO BOOK I.

1. *Hurried away*] It seems to have been the more general opinion that προϊάπτειν necessarily means to send *prematurely* or *untimely;* but I think a little investigation will show that the preposition πρό does not require that special interpretation; and that the meaning of προίαψεν is sufficiently conveyed by the expression "hurried away" (without the addition of either of these adverbs), or by *sent precipitately;* and that, generally speaking, *præmitto,* or *procul mitto,* answers to προϊάπτω. That no such emphasis as has been supposed belongs to the preposition is evident from line 326 of this book, where Agamemnon despatched (προίει, imperf. indic. for προίεε, *præmittebat*) his heralds to Achilles' tent for the purpose of bringing away Briseis; and from lines 116—118 of Book iii., where Hector sends heralds into the city to fetch lambs for sacrifice, while Agamemnon sends to his ships for the like purpose:—προτὶ ἄστυ δύω κήρυκας ἔπεμπε καρπαλίμως being the words used in the former instance, and Ταλθύβιον προίει . . . . νῆας ἔπι γλαφυρὰς ἰέναι in the latter. Here it would be absurd to say that the lambs were untimely or prematurely sent for; and the two expressions—both being used on the same occasion—must be taken as equivalent each to the other. Thus it would appear that Cowper might have avoided the inconvenience of using the adjective "premature" for the corresponding adverb, and that Pope gave himself unnecessary trouble in altering his line (as originally written), for the purpose, as Spence supposed, of introducing the word "untimely." The following is Spence's account of the circumstance :—

"When I was looking on his foul copy of the Iliad, and observing how very much it was corrected and interlined, he said, 'I believe you would find on examination that those parts which have been the most corrected read the easiest.' I read only the first page, in which

. . . . . . ἢ μυρί' 'Αχαιοῖς ἄλγε' ἔθηκε,
Πολλὰς δ' ἰφθίμους ψυχὰς "Αϊδι προίαψεν
'Ηρώων,

was translated —

> ' That strow'd with warriors dead the Phrygian plain,
> And peopled the dark shade with heroes slain.'

It now stands thus,—

> ' That wrath which hurl'd to Pluto's gloomy reign
> The souls of mighty chiefs untimely slain,'—

and was evidently altered to preserve the sense of the word *προύαψεν*."

But I submit that a better reason for the change existed in avoiding the impropriety of speaking of the same persons in the first line as " warriors dead," and in the next as " heroes slain," as if they were distinct and different persons.

2. *Yet was fulfilling, so, the will of Jove*] Cowper's rendering—" So Jove his will perform'd "—does not convey the meaning quite correctly. The verb being in the imperfect tense (*ἐτελείετο*) denotes a design or action not yet fulfilled, but in the process of accomplishment; and the explanation is this : Jove had willed the destruction of Troy; but the quarrel between Agamemnon and Achilles, by bringing so much disaster on the Greeks, seemed to thwart his design : on the contrary, however, this design was all the while being promoted by that apparently counter-acting occurrence ; for during the adverse fortune of the Greeks consequent upon the quarrel, Patroclus, the bosom friend of Achilles, was slain by Hector ; against whom, therefore, Achilles became so enraged as to emerge from his sulky retirement, and (casting aside his resentment of Agamemnon's offence) to enter the field against Hector, the bulwark of Troy ; whom in turn he slew, and thereby turned the fortune of the war, which consequently soon afterwards terminated in the ruin of the capital and the realm of Priam ; and thus the design of Jove, which, all through the vicissitudes of the strife, had in different ways been fulfilling, was eventually fulfilled.

I believe I am justified in considering the expression " yet was fulfilling, so, the will of Jove," as parenthetical, although I am sorry that in so treating it I am not kept in countenance by Lord Derby, who writes,—

> " . . . but so had Jove decreed
> From that sad day when first in wordy war
> The mighty Agamemnon, king of men,
> Confronted stood by Peleus' godlike son "—

as if the decree of Jove dated no farther back than the period of that quarrel. The words *ἐξ οὗ* should be referred to, and taken in connexion with

$$ ἣ \ μυρί' \ Ἀχαιοῖς \ ἄλγε' \ ἔθηκε, \ κ.τ.λ. $$

A close translation of the exordium would be as follows :—
Sing, goddess, the lasting wrath of Achilles, the son of Peleus, *that*
destructive *wrath* which inflicted ten thousand (a large definite put for an
immense number) woes upon the Achæans, and precipitated many brave
souls of heroes to Hades, and made themselves (viz. their bodies) a prey
to dogs and to all devouring birds (yet so was Jove fulfilling his design),
from the time when first Atrides, king of men, and divine Achilles, having
quarrelled, were separated :—which means that the woes to the Greeks
(not the design of Jove) took place from that period or event.

3. *Slow alongside the many-waved sea*] I have not given to πολύ-
φλοισβος the generally-accepted signification of *loud-sounding*, or the like;
thinking, as I do, that it is very questionable whether such is the best, or
even the true meaning of the word as here used by Homer. The verse,

Βῆ δ' ἀκέων παρὰ θῖνα πολυφλοίσβοιο θαλάσσης,

so expressive, as it is imagined, by its melancholy flow, of the bereaved
father's state of mind, and containing in the word in question a supposed
correspondence to the noise of the sea, depends, for much of its effect in
these respects, on the *os rotundum* of the English mode of pronouncing
Greek, by which we give a long intonation to the last syllable in ἀκέων,
and a full sonorous utterance to πολυφλοίσβοιο : but the modern Greeks
(who may be presumed to be most likely right on this point) make, I believe, no difference of pronunciation between the *Omicron* and the *Omega*
(the latter of which was unknown in Homer's age); while they pronounce
πολυφλοίσβοιο in a soft, and fine or mincing manner; and their reading
of the above verse would be (as nearly as it is possible for me to represent
it in English characters)—

Be d' akeon para theena polyfleesveeo thalasses.

Thus the imagined *onomatopeia* is destroyed [1]. Is it not, therefore, probable that φλοῖσβος, as coming from φλέω, refers to the foamy-fringed
waves, as they flow towards and effervesce along the beach ; and, so, is
descriptive of the *appearance* rather than of the *sound* of the sea? as in
Æschyl. Prom. 80,

ποντίων τε κυμάτων
ἀνήριθμον γέλασμα—

a passage which the Author of "The Christian Year" had in his mind
while writing
" When up some woodland dale we catch
The many-twinkling smile of ocean.''

[1] A distinguished authority, to whom the above note 3 had been submitted, on
returning it to the author said, " You are quite right in your statement as to the
modern Greeks' pronunciation ; at the same time it may be observed that, while they
retain the right accent of the language of their forefathers, they have lost the quantity."

Since writing the last paragraph, I have observed that Lord Derby uses the phrase " many-dashing," which, as being applicable in respect of both sound and sight, would, perhaps, be unexceptionable, were it clearly allowable to combine an adjective expressive of multitude with an active participle without an objective case. *Much*-dashing would avoid that doubt, but would not probably be thought either so euphonious, or so poetical.

APPIAN, in his *Halientics*, i. 777, uses φλοῖσβος in the same sense as ἀφρός, *foam*. According to this, *much-foaming* sea would be as eligible a phrase as any that could be invented ; and, had I thought of it at the right time, I think I should have used it in preference to " many-wavèd." However, still retaining this in my preceding version, I will conclude the present topic by here adding, as a various reading,

> " Trembling, the old man fail'd not to obey :
> *Along the shore of the much-foaming sea*
> He silent moved," &c.

4. *Smintheus*] This surname of Apollo has been a subject of much research and disputation ; and the conjectures respecting its derivation are various and conflicting. According as they are differently credited, the appellation may have owed its origin to a town in the Troad called *Sminthea*, or *Sminthus*, sacred to Apollo, or to the word σμίνθα, the Cretan name for *mouse ;* and, in the latter case, the title in question may have been conferred on the god either as a destroyer of mice, or for the quite opposite reason, that those creatures were sacred to him. Schrevelius's Greek and Latin Lexicon contains the following explanation : " Σμινθεύς, *Apollo.* Sic dictus quia cùm Smintham urbem mures infestarent, animalia infesta confecit, cujus memores beneficii, templum et simulacrum Apollini Smintheo posuerunt, et figuram muris ad statuæ pedes expressam." But in a recent edition (Greek and English) of Schrevelius, edited by Rev. J. R. Major, D.D., Head Master of King's College School, London, the city so freed from those animals is called *Chrysa.* On the contrary, in Ainsworth it is called *Sminthia ;* and to the name *Smintheus* there is added this explanation : [" à Smintha, quæ Cretensium linguâ murem domesticum signi."] "A title of Apollo given to him for freeing Sminthia, a colony of the Cretans near the Hellespont, from mice, which much infested them. Ov. Met. xii. 585." On turning to this reference, however (where the above surname of the god appears in the accusative as Sminthea), I find this foot-note :—" Apollinem, *cui mures*, qui linguâ Cretensium σμίνθοι appellantur, *sacri sunt.* Τὰ οὖν περὶ τοὺς Τεύκρους καὶ τοὺς μύας, ἀφ' ὧν ὁ Σμινθεύς, ἐπειδὴ Σμίνθιοι οἱ μύες. *Strabo*, lib. xiii. Sed rationes nominis varias, seu fabulas, lege apud Lil. Gyraldum Syntagm. *Farn.*" Few, if any, however, I presume will care to pursue the inquiry any farther. Moreover, while thus far we are left in doubt on the question whether it is as a destroyer of mice, or as their tutelary deity, that Apollo receives his Sminthean appellation, the following ob-

servations of Richard Payne Knight (which I have met with since the foregoing part of my note was composed) will probably be thought sufficient to show that the title rests on neither of those foundations, and that his argument.amounts to a *quietus* on the subject.

"The omission or insertion of the subsidiary and paragogic N having been left in a great measure to the discretion of transcribers, has, I believe, introduced considerable confusion both in the meaning and etymology of several of Homer's words. .Upon the medals of Alexandria Troas, the title of Apollo, which we now write Σμινθεύς, is uniformly Σμιθεύς, which has so near a resemblance to our word *smith*, and its various derivations, that we cannot but suppose it to have come from the same root, and to have signified the *Smiter*, or *destroyer* generally, according to a well-known attribute of Apollo, expressed in the symbolical writing of ancient art by the bow and arrows which he carried. The tale which deduces it from Σμίνθος, said to have been the Cretan name for a *mouse*, is of later times, and gives a signification unworthy of the solemnity of the occasion on which Chryses invokes the god in his character of Destroyer to avenge his wrongs upon the Greeks."

5. The *thighs* of the animals offered in sacrifice were especially appropriated to the gods, as emblems probably of strength. Cowper does not here mention these, the most essential part of the offering. The *fat*, which alone he specifies, was the adipose membrane called the *caul*, which was doubled or folded over the thighs, with slices or morsels cut from the other parts of the animal, as their representatives, I suppose. The entire thighs, with the caul or fat, and the enveloped representative pieces, were so placed together upon the altar as to be burnt to a flame, and entirely consumed. The rest of the animal served for the feast of the sacrificers, which followed the offering.

The English butchers of the present day are in the practice of covering the thighs (improperly called legs) of lamb with the caul, fastened thereto by skewers.

6. *And not in battle, &c.*] I have interpolated this line, not merely for the purpose of making a rhyme, but also because it is in perfect harmony with the context to represent <u>Minerva</u> as especially grieved at the *kind* of death her heroes were suffering—falling by an ignominious pestilence instead of the weapons of war.

7. Homer every where, so far as I can recollect, mentions Chryseis as a girl, or virgin, where she is not designated by the appellation of *daughter* alone (the term applied to her in other instances being either παῖς or κούρη); whereas I have somewhere read that her proper name was *Astynome* (her other name being derived from her father, Chryses), and that she was the wife of Eëtion, the sovereign of Lyrnessa, upon the

capture of which city by the Greeks, she (as we have seen) fell to Agamemnon, as his share of the spoils. Pope in two places represents this royal lady as subjected to the conqueror's chain. In lines 15 and 16 of his version it is said—

> " For Chryses sought by costly gifts to gain
> His captive daughter from the victor's chain."

And at verses 484 and 485—

> " The priest of Phœbus sought by gifts to gain
> His beauteous daughter from the victor's chain."

It were needless to state that the original poem affords no warrant for this indignity; and there is something revolting in the representation, though it be understood as only figurative of simple captivity. The rhyme thus gained was purchased too dearly.

8. *Though never more, perhaps, I may share her bed*] The insertion of this line will, I trust, be excused, as its prophetic import was fulfilled ; though Agamemnon is not to be supposed to have had any presentiment of the tragical cause of its realization. Not every reader, probably, is acquainted with the fact that this great monarch and supreme leader, on his return home after the destruction of Troy, was murdered by his wife Clytemnestra and her paramour Ægistheus (with whom she, in her husband's absence, had formed an adulterous intercourse). But his cruel fate was avenged by his son Orestes, in putting to death the guilty pair, though she was his own mother ; on account of which he was driven to distraction by the Furies. What was told him by the Oracle at Delphi, in answer to his inquiry as to the means of obtaining release from his affliction, and his proceedings in consequence of the response, would constitute too long a tale for relation here. Upon the story is founded one of the tragedies of Euripides.

9. *Most covetous and vain-glorious of men*] The literal rendering of the words which I have thus translated would be *most glorious and avaricious of all ;* but I have ventured to treat κυδίστη as being spoken ironically, and have therefore rendered it "most *vain*-glorious," which avoids, too, the incongruity that exists between the two epithets when κυδίστη is taken seriously. I like Cowper's free translation—

> " Atrides glorious above all *in rank*,
> And as intent on gain as thou art great "—

since the qualifying words "in rank" get rid of the objection to a serious interpretation, though there is no qualification in the original. Pope is content with the following paraphrase : —

" Insatiate king (Achilles thus replies),
Fond of the pow'r, but fonder of the prize."

10. It seems strange that one great military chief should make it a matter of reproach to another that he is fond of *war*, the special occupation of both. I have therefore prefixed to the noun the adjective *wordy*, which in sense agrees with the context; the whole imputation having relation to the alleged propensity of Achilles to quarrelling.

11. *While thus distracted in his mind and soul*] (. . . . κατὰ φρένα καὶ κατὰ θυμόν.) The words φρένα and θυμόν are doubtless used distinctively, to represent respectively the seats of reason and of passion.

12. It appears not to have occurred to Homer, that if it was expedient to render Minerva invisible to all the assembly except Achilles, it was equally so to render both her and him inaudible to the rest; or that, as she was invisible to all but him, she might as well have placed herself face to face before him, instead of pulling his hair from behind, and so causing him to turn round and address his " wingèd words " to seeming vacuity (while, in consequence of it, a pause was taking place in the altercation between him and Agamemnon), to the amazement, one would think, of the king and the other bystanders. The anticipated answer that the scene is only an allegory, designed to represent a conflict in the mind of Achilles (ending in the eventual predominance of his prudence over his passion), does not exclude the objection, that the circumstances, though figurative, should be as free from absurdity as they would be expected to appear if they were real.

13. *Doubtless, sage Nestor . . . .*] The appellation in the text which I have thus rendered is there simply γέρον (in the vocative), *old man*, an expression of veneration in those days. Cowper renders it *old chief;* while Pope makes the king, without using any appellation, begin his reply to the sage by telling him that he is awfully old :

" Thy years are awful, and thy words are wise."

14. *The robbery of the girl I'll not resist*] It might, at first sight, seem inconsistent in Achilles, not only not to make any physical resistance to the seizure of Briseis by Agamemnon, after so much wordy opposition, but also to tell him that he will not resist the robbery of this his most cherished possession, and, in making the renunciation, to allude to her with apparent slight by designating her as " the girl," while he defies him, on pain of death, to take any of his " other things," as if he valued those more than her : and this defiance looks like the empty bravado of one who threatens his adversary with the consequence of doing what he knows there is no danger of being done. But, on the other hand, it may

be supposed that Achilles in his non-resistance was actuated by the desire of averting as speedily as possible the destructive plague, the cessation of which depended upon the restitution of Chryseis, whom he knew Agamemnon would not surrender without the substitution of Briseis. Or, without giving Achilles credit for that generous and self-denying sentiment, we may imagine him to have been influenced by the consideration that the army (whose safety was thus at stake) would not support him in his resistance, if any such he should make; and their standing aloof from him in the contest supplied him with a motive for including them with Agamemnon in his fatal resentment. I am not aware that thoughts similar to these have before occurred to any commentator; but I find upon the passage under notice, in Pope's version, the following note, after the words—

> ". . . . No more Achilles draws
> His conqu'ring sword in any woman's cause "

(which, by the way, do not correspond to the language of the text) :—

" When Achilles promises not to contest for Briseis, he expresses it in a sharp, despising air : *I will not fight for the sake of a woman ;* by which he glances at Helena, and casts an oblique reflection upon those commanders whom he is about to leave at the siege for her cause. One may observe how well it is fancied of the poet to make one woman the ground of a quarrel which breaks an alliance that was only formed [*sic,* for formed only] on account of another [woman], and how much the circumstances thus considered contribute to keep up the anger of Achilles for carrying on the poem beyond the dissolution of the council. For (as he himself argues with Ulysses in the ninth Iliad) it is as reasonable for him to retain his anger on account of Briseis, as for the brothers, with all Greece, to carry on a war on the score of Helen."

There are two or three circumstances attending the departure of Briseis from the tent of Achilles to that of her new lord which seem to me well worthy of particular regard. When the heralds arrive to fetch her, Achilles does not himself venture into his tent to take leave of her, and in so doing run the risk of creating a scene unbecoming his dignity; but he devolves the task of preparing her for the unwelcome change upon his distinguished friend Patroclus,—not upon any inferior officer; thus showing her every consideration that the case would admit of; and when she is brought forth, and, in going with the heralds, passes near the spot where he is sitting in the open air, it does not appear that he directs a glance towards her. I have beheld the scene beautifully imagined in a picture, where, while being led away by the heralds, one on each side of her, she as she walks (almost dragged) reluctantly forward, twists back her form, and turns her head with tearful eyes towards her loved hero, as if trying to catch a parting look from him; he at the same time, with gloomy and sorrowful aspect, gazing away in a different direction.

15. In one and the same line of the text, the sea, under the several names of ἅλς and πόντος, is characterized as simultaneously *hoary* in the first case, and *dark* (purple, or wine-faced) in the other: ἁλὸς πολιῆς and οἴνοπα πόντον. Those different aspects must therefore be referred to different parts of the sea. Near the shore, where Achilles was sitting, the foamy fringes, or crests of the crisped waves, would entitle the surface to the first epithet; while the second would belong to the expanse of the distant deep, to which he was directing his contemplation, and where the hoary edges of the billows vanish from the view. To suit this predicament I have inserted the word "near" relative to the situation of Achilles, and the word "beyond" in reference to his extended vision.

> Then did Achilles on the tent-strewn shore,
> Where the near sea a hoary surface wore,
> Looking beyond upon the purple deep,
> Apart from his associates, sit to weep;
> And there, with arms outstretch'd, and hands display'd,
> To his fond mother fervently he pray'd.

Cowper evades πολιῆς altogether, and translates οἴνοπα "gloomy." Pope notices neither the one colour nor the other; but disposes of the case in these lines:—

> "Not so his loss the fierce Achilles bore;
> But sad retiring to the sandy shore,
> O'er the wild margin of the deep he hung,
> The kindred deep from which his mother sprung;
> There, bathed in tears of anger and disdain,
> Thus loud lamented to the stormy main."

This rendering is objectionable in respect both of redundancy and of omission; and presents one of the numerous instances in which the translator makes every thing give way to beautiful versification. While he omits noticing either of the aspects of the sea, he *gratuitously* alludes to the hero's relationship to it, as being both kindred and his mother's birthplace; at the same time representing him (instead of *praying* to *her*, according to the text) as *lamenting* to *it* under the changed name of "the stormy main." There is, however, appended to this passage, in my copy of Pope's version, a note which may be thought worth transcribing:—

" *There, bathed in tears*] Eustathius observes on this place that it is no weakness in heroes to weep, but the very effect of humanity, and proof of a generous temper, for which he offers several instances, and takes notice that if Sophocles would not let Ajax weep, it is because he is drawn rather as a madman than a hero. But this general observation is not all he can offer in excuse for the tears of Achilles: his are tears of anger and disdain (as I have ventured to call them in the translation) of which a great and fiery temper is more susceptible than any other; and, even in this case,

Homer has taken care to preserve the high character of Achilles, by making him retire to vent his tears out of sight. And we may add to these an observation of which Madame Dacier is fond. The reason why Agamemnon parts not in tears from Chryseis, as Achilles does from Briseis, is: the one parts willingly with his mistress; and, because he does it for his people's safety, it becomes an honour to him: and the other is parted unwillingly; and, because his general takes her away by force, the action reflects dishonour upon him."

But, begging pardon of Madame Dacier's memory, I take the liberty of differing from her in reference to the compliment she pays Agamemnon, who appears to me quite undeserving of any commendation on this occasion. With all his affected regard for his people's safety, he would not resign his "mistress" without receiving "an equivalent" suited to his taste, though this was to be obtained only by robbery.

As an instance of the hold which this matchless production takes on the mind of the reader, he feels almost as glad on finding, in the sequel, Briseis restored inviolate to Achilles, as one could be if the fiction were a reality.

16. Cowper labours under a grand mistake in applying to *Neptune* a remark in the text which relates to *Ægeon,* alias *Briareus.* The words Ὅς ῥα παρὰ Κρονίων καθέζετο κύδεϊ γαίων are spoken of Ægeon after the performance of his exploit; not of his father Neptune, whom he excelled in strength and defeated with the other rebellious gods. I can imagine that Cowper was misled by the circumstance that the immediately antecedent noun to ὅς is πατρός. But ὅς is preceded by a full stop, and evidently relates to the *remoter* antecedent (Ægeon), both antecedents being in the same clause, or member, of the preceding sentence.

Αἰγείων· ὃ γὰρ αὖτε βίῃ οὗ πατρὸς ἀμείνων·
Ὅς ῥα κ.τ.λ.

Cowper's rendering of the whole passage is this:—

" For I, not seldom, in my father's hall,
    Have heard thee boasting, how when once the gods,
    With Juno, Neptune, Pallas, at their head,
    Conspired to bind the Thund'rer, thou didst loose
    His bands, O goddess, calling to his aid
    The hundred-handed warrior, by the gods
    Briareus, but by men Ægeon, named.
    For he in prowess and in might surpass'd
    His father, Neptune, *who, enthroned sublime,*
    Sits, second only to Saturnian Jove
    In joy and glory."

There are not in the original any words applied to Neptune at all corresponding to

"Who, enthroned sublime,
Sits, second only to Saturnian Jove
In joy and glory."

That the little of those which bears any resemblance to the text relates, or rather should have been made to relate, to Ægeon is further proved by the particle ῥα, and by the tense of the verb, καθέζετο, the imperfect Ionic; whereas Cowper changes it into the present, "sits." It is to be presumed that the monster *sat* for a short time only, to exult in his superior strength and enjoy his triumph; and then went about his own business, which it has been supposed was that of piracy on a grand scale; his hundred hands and fifty heads being, it is thought, emblematical of the forces under his command. His seafaring occupation would bring him into acquaintance-ship with Thetis, and subject him to her beck and call.

17. There has been a diversity of opinion as to whether by Ὠκεανός Homer meant a *river* of that name (which some suppose to be the same which is now called the Nile), or the *ocean*. The only definition of it given in "Brasse's Greek Gradus" is *oceanus*, the ocean, with the synonyms θάλασσα, πόντος, ἀμφιτρίτη: while "Dymock's Bibliotheca Classica" states that Homerus uses it to signify the Nile, citing for an example (not the instance now in question, but) Od. xxiv. 11. According to one mythological account, the name was originally given to the eldest son of *Cœlus* and *Terra*, who married Thetis, by whom, it is said, he had three thousand beautiful daughters. The word afterwards (it is added) became (but by what process does not appear) the name of any immense expanse of salt water. Justinus uses it in one place to signify the Indian Sea, and in another the Mediterranean. In reference to the supposition that by "ocean" Homer meant the Nile, Herodotus says he knows no river named Oceanus, and he thinks that Homer, or some earlier poet, invented the name, and put it into his works. I add the words from the text of Herodotus:—Οὐ γάρ τινα ἔγωγε οἶδα ποταμὸν Ὠκεανὸν ἐόντα. Ὅμηρον δὲ ἤ τινα τῶν πρότερον γενομένων ποιητέων, δοκέω τὸ ὄνομα εὑρόντα ἐς τὴν ποίησιν ἐσενείκασθαι (Book ii. 23). Whether Homer meant a river or the ocean, the etymology agrees with both; since ὠκέα (for ὠκεῖα) and νάω are applicable to the current of the one and to the tide of the other.

For ἀμύμονας some commentators have read Μέμνονας, as if the Ethiopians had derived this denomination by gift from *Memnon*; but it seems more reasonable to ascribe the epithet to their pious or religious character, in reference to their distinguished veneration for Jupiter especially, with the other gods, and to the pomps and ceremonies that characterized their worship. "Among these was an annual feast at Diospolis, which Eustathius mentions, in which they carried about the statues of Jupiter and the other gods for twelve days, according to their number: to which if we add the ancient custom of setting meat before statues, it will appear a rite from which this fable might easily rise."

These religious rites supplied to me the motive for translating ἀμύμων into "pious," as being, on account of the positive or active virtue implied by this word, more *ad rem* than the passive or negative merit signified by the primary meaning and more common reading of *blameless*, or *innocent*. Pope, however, has adopted "blameless ;" while Cowper has not thought it worth while to take any notice of either their piety or their innocence.

18. It is difficult to conceive what motive Homer could have had for placing Jupiter upon the highest peak of snowy Olympus immediately on his return from the hot climate of Ethiopia. Such a conspicuous spot, too, was most inconvenient for his *tête-à-tête* with Thetis.

19. The following extract from Dr. Blair's "Lectures on Rhetoric and Belles Lettres," may, I think, be aptly introduced here.

" Homer's description of this nod of Jupiter as shaking the heavens, has been admired in all ages as highly sublime. Literally translated it runs thus: ' He spoke, and, bending his sable brows, gave the awful nod ; while he shook the celestial locks of his immortal head, all Olympus was shaken.' Mr. Pope translates it thus :—

> ' He spoke, and awful bends his sable brows,
> Shakes his ambrosial curls, and gives the nod,
> The stamp of fate, and sanction of a god.
> High heav'n with trembling the dread signal took,
> And all Olympus to the centre shook.'

The image is spread out and attempted to be beautified, but it is in truth weakened. The third line, ' The stamp of fate, and sanction of a god,' is merely expletive, and introduced for no other reason but to fill up the rhyme; for it interrupts the description and clogs the image. For the same reason, one of mere compliance with the rhyme, Jupiter is represented as shaking his locks before he gives the nod ; ' shakes his ambrosial locks, and gives the nod ;' which is trifling, and without meaning : whereas, in the original, the hair of the head shaken is the effect of the nod, and makes a happy, picturesque circumstance."

But however just these remarks are in substance, other critics may think that the criticism itself is not free from several inaccuracies of expression.

20. *During the day continued my descent*] How is this descent of Vulcan, long in point of time, to be reconciled with the comparatively low elevation of Olympus (only 6000 feet), or with the rapid transit of

Jupiter and his train to and from Ethiopia, or, again, with that of Thetis, on their return, following them from the sea, and her passage back by a single bound—without particularizing other examples of instantaneous transition by Minerva and other celestials in different parts of the poem? From the circumstance that the summit was often enveloped in clouds, the ancients, or their poets at least, supposed that it touched the heavens, and therefore they imagined it to be the residence of the gods; while by those poets Olympus was used as synonymous with *cælum* itself. Besides, it does not, so far as I can recollect, appear that Homer any where mentions any other locality than that of this mountain as one of the celestial abodes. Still, when Vulcan kept falling

"From morn till dewy eve, a summer's day,"

it must (in order to get over the inconsistency alluded to) be supposed that the gods were then occupying some far loftier region than the one in question.

It is interesting to notice what vague and incongruous, yet often grand conceptions the ancient pagans of different nations entertained relative to the abodes of their divinities,—all of them however connected with the idea of altitude, and such as a knowledge of the earth's spherical form, and of the antipodes with *their* heaven, would have destroyed. Yet amid the variety, a certain degree of similarity attached to them all.

"It is observed by Sir William Jones," says Dugald Stewart, in his "Essay on the Sublime," "that the Jupiter, or Diespiter, mentioned by Ennius, in the line,

'Aspice hoc sublime candens quem invocant Jovem,'

is the Indian God of the visible heavens, called *Indra*, or the *King*, and *Diespiter*, or Lord of the Sky; and that most of his epithets in Sanscrit, are the same with those of *Ennian Jove;* . . . . and though the East is particularly under his care, yet his Olympus is *Meru*, or the North Pole, allegorically represented as a mountain of gold and gems,"—a seat assuredly preferable to a mountain clothed with snow and capped with clouds.

I cannot resist the temptation to add the following passage transcribed from the essay just alluded to, although it is but remotely connected with our subject:—

"Is it not probable that the impression produced by this association (*altitude* and *sublimity*), strong as it still is, was still stronger in ancient times? The discovery of the earth's sphericity, and of the general theory of gravitation, has taught us that the words *above* and *below* have only a relative import. The natural association cannot fail to be more or less counteracted in every understanding to which the doctrine is familiarized; and though it may not be *so far* weakened as to destroy altogether the effect of poetical description proceeding on popular phraseology, the effect

H

must necessarily be inferior to what it was in ages when the notions of the wise concerning the local residence of the gods were precisely the same with those of the vulgar. We may trace their powerful influence on the philosophy of Plato in some of his dialogues ; and he is deeply indebted to them for that strain of sublimity which characterizes those parts of his writings which have more peculiarly excited the enthusiasm of his followers."

With due respect, however, for the opinion of such a distinguished philosopher and metaphysician as Dugald Stewart, I am inclined to think that Plato's sublime conceptions and feelings would have been heightened and intensified by an acquaintance with the vast discoveries made by astronomers since his time. What a small part of even the known universe is indicated by the example, that if ten inches were made to represent the mean radius of the earth's annual orbit (the diameter of this orbit being a line of 195,000,000 of miles in length), then a triangle with the aforesaid base (ten inches), and sides 300 miles long, would represent relatively the distance from the earth to one of the nearest fixed stars ! Or, proximately, as ten inches are to 300 miles, so is the mean radius (say about 95,000,000 of miles) of the earth's orbit to the distance of the earth from such a star ! Then, for an illustration of distance and magnitude combined,—supposing the whole of that orbit filled up with a globe as bright as the sun, it would have a circumference of 600,000,000 of miles, and yet appear as only a twinkling point when seen from the nearest of the fixed stars !

The curious extract which I now subjoin, from a letter written by Sir James Macintosh, when Governor of Bombay, to Stewart, appears to point to an era of enlightenment in ages long anterior to the introduction of the gross and superstitious mythology in his day, and still existing in India, and as far remote, perhaps, from the first growth of the more elegant theological system recognized in Homer's time ;—to an era, indeed, when there existed a system at once philosophical and theological ; being the same, I presume, with the Vedanta doctrine which Sir William Jones had characterized as " *a system wholly built on the purest devotion.*"

" I had yesterday," says Sir James, " a conversation with a young Brahmin of no great learning, the son of the Pundit (or assessor for Hindu law) of my court. He told me that besides the myriads of gods whom their creed admits, there was one whom they knew by the name of BRIM, or the Great One, without form or limits, whom no created intellect could make any approach towards conceiving ;—that in reality there were no trees, no houses, no land, no sea, but all without was *maia*, or illusion, the act of BRIM ;—that whatever we saw or felt was only a dream, or, as he expressed it in his imperfect English, *thinking in one's sleep ;* and that the reunion of the soul to BRIM, from whom it originally sprung, was *the awakening from the long sleep of finite existence.* All

this you have heard and read before. What struck me was that specula-
tions so refined and abstruse should, in a long course of years, have fallen
through so great a space as that which separates the genius of their
original inventors from the mind of this weak and unlettered man. The
names of those inventors have perished, but their ingenious and beautiful
theories, blended with the most monstrous superstitions, have descended
to men very little exalted above the most ignorant populace, and are
adopted by them as a sort of articles of faith, without a suspicion of their
philosophical origin, and without the possibility of their comprehending
any part of the premises from which they were deduced. I intend to
investigate a little the history of these opinions², for I am not altogether
without apprehension that we may all the while be mistaking the hyperboli-
cal effusions of mystical piety for the technical language of a philosophical
system. Nothing is more usual than for fervent devotion to dwell so
long and so warmly on the meanness and the worthlessness of created
things, and on the all-sufficiency of the Supreme Being, that it slides
insensibly from comparative to absolute language, and in the eagerness
of its zeal to magnify the deity, seems to *annihilate* every thing else.
To distinguish between the very different import of the same words in
the mouth of a mystic and a sceptic requires more philosophical discrimi-
nation than most of our Sanscrit investigators have hitherto shown."

21. *Th' immortals to their sep'rate halls retired*] Cowper has, in the
corresponding passage of his version, introduced the words "wheresoever
built," and *not unaptly* (though there is nothing of the sort in the original);
for it is difficult to imagine where they could be in a region so ill adapted,
as one would think, both for sleeping and banqueting.

22. . . . . *a short time slept*] I had inserted these words to reconcile a
supposed contradiction in the original between the close of the first book
and the opening of the second ere I discovered that *Eustathius* makes
this distinction between ὑπνοῦν and καθεύδειν, that the latter may or does
mean *to lie down in a disposition to sleep*, without actually sleeping.
But as no lexicon in my possession recognizes this interpretation, I suffer
my interpolation to remain. One lexicon, indeed (Donegan's), to the
generally received significations of καθεύδειν adds this peculiar one,—*to be
free from care*. Now, if Jove did not sleep, it was owing to his *indispo-
sition* to sleep, because he was disturbed by care. But the words in the
second line of book ii. do not assert that Jove had *no* sleep : they merely
say that sweet sleep did not hold him, or retain possession of him :—

Δία δ' οὐκ ἔχε νήδυμος ὕπνος·

² The result of the investigation (if, in fact, the intention was ever acted upon) has
never come to my knowledge.

H 2

while it is stated that the other gods slept all night, εὗδον παννύχιοι. The predicament, however, is met by allowing him to have taken a short nap at the end of the first book, and suffering sleep to forsake him at the beginning of the second. By adding that "Juno, near him laid, *no vigil kept,*" I have made a seasonable allusion to her watching propensity (for which, in the course of the preceding day, she had received such a severe reprimand) answer the purpose of completing the rhyme.

NOTES TO BOOK II.

1. *In this guise, therefore, did the Dream divine*] To term a delusive or treacherous dream divine, may seem out of character; but in relation to its author it is not so. At any rate the word corresponds to the original (θεῖος) epithet in this place applied to it, though it is previously termed (in the vocative case) οὖλε ὄνειρε, baneful dream. Thus Jupiter addresses it in a bad sense, while the poet hallows its name in relating the commission entrusted to it as the messenger of the divinity. Pope's description of the transaction is so curious that I am induced to transcribe it.

> " Swift as the word the vain illusion fled,
> Descends, and hovers o'er Atrides' head :
> Clothed in the figure of the Pylean sage
> Renown'd for wisdom and revered for age ;
> Around his temples spreads his golden wing,
> And thus the flatt'ring Dream deceives the king."

Here the vain illusion, though it has assumed the form of Nestor, represents the old man with a golden wing, which he spreads round " *his* temples ;" but those of the *king* (who is subsequently mentioned) are, I presume, meant ; though this does not appear perfectly clear. The circumstance of the pronoun " his " appearing twice in the same line—first in connexion with the temples, and secondly with the wing—renders it questionable whether *both* the *his's* refer to Nestor, or the one to him and his wing, and the other to Agamemnon (over whose head the disguised dream is hovering) and his (Agamemnon's) temples. While I suppose the general opinion would incline to the latter interpretation, the more rigid rules of construction would sanction the other. Amidst the confusion to which the third person of pronouns is (in the English language especially) liable, the sense is generally sufficient for directing the application of them to their proper nouns respectively ; but here the sense itself is too ambiguous to be a certain guide. Whether, however, the pretended Nestor's temples, or the monarch's, are meant, the features of the former would, one should imagine, be concealed from the latter by the intervention of the surrounding wing; and thus the Nestorian guise (*plus* the wing), whatever might have been the reason for inventing the counterfeit, would have been assumed superfluously and in vain. As the case stands, the wing, which shaded the temples of one or the other of the parties, answers no other end than that of overshadowing the meaning with doubt, and making a rhyme to "king." Had Pope made the noun "dream" of the neuter gender, and so used the genitive case *its* in relation to it, he would have avoided the awkward repetition of "his" and the consequent ambiguity. It would not be a sufficient answer to say that Homer has used the masculine form ὄνειρος, there being also a neuter form ὄνειρον, and both having the same theme,—ὄναρ, τό. Besides, a translator is not, in all cases, bound to adhere to the genders of the original. Such an obligation would make it incumbent on him, in translating from the German, to speak of the sun as *she*, and of the moon as *he*.

If Dr. Blair thought it no waste of time to make such a long comment as I lately transcribed from one of his works into a preceding note, upon the circumstance of a *misplaced nod*, I hope it will not be thought that I have been excessively prodigal of that invaluable commodity in my remarks upon the unwarranted creation of an unnatural wing.

2. This tradition is related by Pausanias, ix. 19. The cow having at this place met and *bellowed* (ἐμυκήσατο) to Cadmus and his companions, guided them to the spot they were in search of. That non-Grecian readers may understand the connexion alluded to, they are informed that the verb, which in the tense here quoted is translated "having bellowed," or "lowed," is in its first person present (expressed in English characters) *mucaō*, or *mucō*; but in translating, the *u* is changed into *y*: hence Mycalessus.

3. *High-raised Hyampolis*] Preparatory to the few remarks which I shall have occasion to make in reference to some of the different places which contributed their several forces to the war on either side, I think it expedient to deprecate any expectation of finding those places noticed always in the same order in which they occur in the original poem. This would be quite impossible in versification of any kind, and particularly so in rhyme, where a double restraint exists; nor would it with more reason be expected that different translations should in this respect coincide with one another, any more than with the original. It is sufficient if all the places be found in their proper groups; and while I believe that I have not omitted a single place, nor the name of any leader, I hope that my transpositions will be found neither more numerous, nor on the whole less congruous than those of any other

translator. The task of transferring a series of proper names from a poem in one language into a version of the same poem in another language, may be compared to building a new house with the stones of another; in doing which the builder is to use every one of those stones, or, at least, corresponding ones, although the different order or style of the new structure renders it impossible to place them in the same relative position which they respectively occupied in the original pile; and as in the new edifice the adding here and there of a new stone or two, or the insertion of a little cement in certain interstices, is allowable, so in a translation a few *callidæ juncturæ* must take place, by the introduction now and then of a gratuitous epithet, and, occasionally, a little circumlocution; care being taken that those added epithets, &c., be such as are warranted by the known character of the persons or places, or justified by their biography, geography, or history. With regard to the new or additional epithets, I think I have never offended against the conditions stated, nor resorted to the expedient oftener than others have done; and though my circumlocutions may be rather more profuse than those of former translators, I flatter myself that they will be found in perfect keeping with the text, while some of them possess the character of embodied notes. In all, or most, instances of any importance, I have distinguished the additions by italic type; and as an example of the liberties taken by me in the respects above mentioned, I will first give a close description, in prose, of the component parts of the Phocenean forces, and then subjoin my rhymic version of the same passage; which I adduce as being, I think, the most extravagant of all my meanderings.

Those who held [inhabited] Cyparissa, and rocky Python, Crissa very divine, and Daulis, and Panopea, and those who dwelt about Anemorea and Hyampolis; and those who dwelt near the sacred river Cephissus; and those who inhabited Lilæa at the fount of Cephissus; with them together forty black ships followed [viz. their leaders previously named].

> " Issued from Cyparissa, and the rocks
> Of Python (destitute of herds and flocks),
> Crissa divine, Daulis, Panopea,
> *High-raised* Hyampolis, and Anemorea,
> Added to those who nigh the noble stream
> Cephissus named (*whose sacred waters gleam*
> *Through rich Bœotia in their beauteous course*)
> Were wont to dwell; and where that river's source
> Is found,—Lilæa, fountain of fair fame:
> This race in forty ships together came."

Here, in the fourth line, being in want of two syllables to place before Hyampolis (which stands without an epithet in the text), I examined every book in my library that I thought likely to afford me some specific

description or character of that place, but in vain until I came to
Wordsworth's "Greece." This informed me that the city in question
was situate on the hill of Acontium, and consequently I felt justified
in applying to it the term "high-raised." In the next place, with the
aid of the same work, I was enabled to trace the course of the Cephissus,
and thus to make a little circumambulation which procured me at once
a rhyme for the river's before-mentioned stream, and another for its
after-mentioned source.

But I cannot part from the last topic without expressing a wish that
every reader of this note who is not already familiar with Wordsworth's
"Greece," might participate in the pleasure which I felt in reading the
Bishop's description of those and other localities therein specified, and in
contemplating the exquisitely beautiful engravings with which Mr. Mur-
ray's recent edition of that work is decorated. Of these I cannot impart
any adequate idea; but a specimen of the verbal painting, or written composition, may be seen in the following extract, relating to the very places
which were the objects of my research, the quotation of which I trust his
lordship will pardon if ever it shall come under his notice :—

"On the western side of Mount Ptoum rises the hill of Acontium,
which is the eastern barrier of the vale of Cephissus. On it are the
remains of the ancient cities of ABÆ and HYAMPOLIS. Beneath its
western foot the river Cephissus runs through rich and beautiful pastures,
corn-fields, and olive-yards, into the Cephissean Lake. Over the other or
western side of the stream hang the steep eminences of Licoreia, consisting
of dark marble cliffs, capped with snow, which are the eastern projections
of MOUNT PARNASSUS. Beneath them is the craggy hill of Daulis, lying
in the fork between two streams, which water the vine-clad slopes of the
valley below it; and then, having united their waters at the eastern foot,
flow together into the channel of the Cephissus.

"From this point commences the long range of HELICON, which
stretches on till it sinks down in a declivity near the city of THESPIÆ,
and the plain of Leuctræ. Through this valley a river flows to the south-
west into the Corinthian Gulf, being the only stream of Bœotia which
discharges its waters there."

4. The word μιν, being an undeclineable accusative, signifying both *him*
and *her*, has afforded an opportunity to commentators and translators for
differing as to its right application; some referring it to PALLAS, others
to ERECTHEUS. The majority, I believe (and, as I think, with good
reason), apply it to Pallas. To represent the Athenians as sacrificing,
in the temple of the goddess, to her *protégé* rather than to herself, seems
quite preposterous.

5. *And the repute of a good king maintain'd*] This expletive line
corresponds to the character of Adrastus, as described by Statius.

6. The *Tegeates*, it is said, were brave and warlike from necessity; their town being situated between the hostile territories of Lacedemon and Manteneia.

7. *Nisyrus, Casus, Crapathus, and Cos*] This line is identical with Cowper's; being the only one of my version, so far as I am aware, that is so, or with a line of any other translator.

Such a correspondence one might imagine to be almost unavoidable in this instance, where the parallel part of the text consists entirely of proper names and conjunctions. Nevertheless the only other versions that I am acquainted with differ considerably even here. Pope, indeed, names the places in the above order, but with the interpolation of adjectives, while, for rhythm, he unwarrantably shortens the penult of Nisyrus. Thus—

> " With them the youth of Nisy̆rus repair,
>   Casus *the strong*, and Crapathus *the fair;*
>   Cos " . . . . . .

Lord Derby designates Cos (the seat of Eurytylus's government) as a *fortress*, and gives the adjective of Casus instead of the noun, by taking this out of the first-mentioned group and connecting it with the second, under the description of " the Casian and Calydnian Isles."

> " Who in Nisyrus dwelt, and *Car*pathus [*sic*],
>   And Cos, the fortress of Eurytylus,
>   And in the Casian and Calydnian Isles—"

Although πόλις has the secondary or remoter meaning of " fortress," or citadel, its primary and more common meaning is (as every reader of Greek knows) *city*, or *state;* and I respectfully submit that the original and general meaning of any word ought not to be departed from unless there be an apparent reason for a special interpretation. In the present case I can see no ground for calling the city of Cos a fortress.

8. *Except those Myrmidons, &c.*] These two gratuitous lines (not wanted for my own convenience) I have introduced solely for the purpose of supplying a manifest *hiatus* in the original poem. Without some such auxiliary, there would be, according to the letter of the text, an absolute contradiction, which will thus appear. After the enumeration of the various Grecian forces, and of their ships and leaders, the poem goes on to describe the inactivity of Achilles and his followers; representing his soldiers as amusing themselves in sportive exercises, and his charioteers as idly wandering about the camp, and regretting the retirement of their chief. Then follows, *immediately, and without any distinction but a full stop*, what is doubtless meant for a description of the hasty and noisy march of the *general army* of Greeks, though their only designation is

the article *oí*, or the relative pronoun *oĩ* (some copies having the one, and some the other), which being rendered by *the* pronoun *they*, or *who*, would in either case, strictly construed, relate to the inactive Myrmidons, whose description (occupying no less than five lines) immediately precedes, and thus intercepts the communication between the pronoun, or article, and the remoter antecedent to which it belongs. I have, therefore, commenced the account of the grand march with the exceptive lines referred to at the head of this note. Cowper takes no notice of the incongruity, and adheres strictly to the text, by using the pronoun *they* alone, without any regard to its relation. Pope uses, instead of the unfathered pronoun, the words " the shining armies ;" but the use of this noun in the plural is open to the objection that it might imply *both* of the opposing hosts ; whereas the Trojan army and their movement are described afterwards. I must add Pope's glowing paraphrase :—

> " Now, like a deluge cov'ring all around,
> The shining armies sweep along the ground ;
> Swift as a flood of fire when storms arise,
> Floats the wide field, and blazes to the skies.
> Earth groans beneath them ; as when angry Jove
> Hurls down the forky lightnings from above,
> On Arimè, when he the thunder throws,
> And fires Typhœus with redoubled blows ;
> Where Typhon, prest beneath the burning load,
> Still feels the fury of th' avenging god."

I am sorry that I do not feel at liberty to quote Lord Derby's far preferable version of the passage under consideration ; but I may be allowed to remark that it begins with the line,

> " Such was the host which like devouring fire," . . .

although, as before observed, the last preceding five lines of the original are employed in describing the continued retirement of Achilles, with the idle state and amusements of his followers.

9. The situation of Arimè, or Arima, is not determined with certainty. Some authors understand the name to designate a place in Cilicia (a country on the south-east coast of Asia Minor) abounding in subterranean fires. Others assert that it was in Syria. But neither of these places would answer to the required locality, if Typhon's mountain-bed was, as generally understood, Mount Etna.

To those who are not extensively acquainted with the mythological rubbish with which classical lore, especially its poetry, is encumbered, some account of the monster Typhon may be acceptable, in order to their understanding the allusion to him in the lastly noticed passage.

And since the great Lord Bacon did not consider it beneath the dignity
of his mighty mind to devote to this subject a whole chapter of his book
"*De Sapientiâ Veterorum*," I may hope to be exempt from the charge of
having trifled away time in making the following translation from a passage
in that work :—

"The poets relate that Juno, being angry because Jupiter had of himself, and without her co-operation, brought forth Pallas, urged all the
[other] gods and goddesses to consent that she herself, without the aid
of Jove, should produce a birth ; and after they had yielded to her violence and importunity, she struck the earth, from whose agitation Typhon
was born :—a huge monster, who was given to a serpent, as his nurse and
guardian, to be brought up. No sooner had he arrived at adolescence,
than he waged war against Jupiter. In that conflict Jupiter came into
the power of the giant, who, having upon his shoulders carried him into a
remote and obscure region, cut the sinews of his hands and feet, and then,
carrying them off with himself, left Jove there maimed and mutilated.
But Mercury, having afterwards stolen the sinews, which Typhon had
carried away, restored them to Jove. Thereupon Jupiter, confirmed in
strength, in his turn attacked Typhon, and with a thunderbolt wounded
the giant, from whose blood serpents were born. Then, at length, having
thrown Etna upon him in his flight, he pressed him down with the mass
of the mountain [which then became a volcano]."

This fable, Bacon observes, was invented concerning the various fortunes
of kings, and the rebellions which in monarchies were sometimes accustomed to happen ; and he proceeds to illustrate the meaning and moral of
the tale ; assigning to all the monstrosities of the giant's horrible figure
(which are successively alluded to) their respective significations. But all
this would be out of place here.

10. *In Ida's dells*] Cowper, in his version, at this place uses the word
"vales." But κνημός means properly *the part of a mountain ascending
from its foot*, and may be aptly represented by *skirt, lap*, or *breast*.
There seems to be an impropriety in speaking of the vales of a mountain.
Little *valleys*, in contradistinction to vales, it may have, since the latter
word implies, I think, a far wider expanse than the former. For example,
I reside on the brow of a range of hills forming one side of a *valley* (so
called), which opens out into a *vale* (thus named) expanding to a breadth
of many square miles. Webster's Dictionary states that "vale" is used in
poetry, and "valley" in prose, as if that distinction (if such really exists)
were the only one ; but the general understanding, or usage, allows, I
believe, the distinction which I have claimed, even in prose. However
that may be, I expect that "dells" will in this case be considered the
most appropriate word ; as those little hollows which are understood by
it are frequent in mountains, and afford convenient nestling-places for the
purpose alluded to in the text. Pope mentions neither vales nor valleys,

nor yet dells; but for Ἴδης ἐν κνημοῖσι uses the phrase "in the shades of Ida's sacred grove." Lord Derby's words in the same place are "amid Ida's jutting peaks."

11. *Where Axius broad and ever beauteous flows*] The words which I have here somewhat freely translated, are

εὐρὺ ῥέοντος
'Αξιοῦ οὗ κάλλιστον ὕδωρ ἐπικίδναται αἴῃ,

But, according to Strabo, so far is the water of the Axius from being entitled to the character of κάλλιστον, that he calls it a muddy river, though its tributary streams are clear. In this respect, therefore, it resembles "the yellow Rhine" receiving "the blue Moselle," whose azure vein may, from the heights of Ehrenbreitstein, be traced, with gradually diminishing distinctness, to a considerable distance from the first point of confluence, ere it becomes completely mingled.

Pope thus copiously amplifies the description of the already ample Axius :—

> " From Axius' ample bed he leads them on,
> Axius that laves the distant Amydon,
> Axius that swells with all its neighb'ring rills,
> And wide around the floating region fills." . . . .

Whereby, it cannot be denied, he gives full force and scope to ἐπικίδναται.

12. *Marshall'd by Nastes and Amphimachus*] Homer's account of the leaders of the Carians is an ambiguous jumble. It first asserts that Nastes led them, next that their leaders were Amphimachus and Nastes, and, thirdly, repeating their names, but in reverse order, adds that they were the sons of Nomion, *who* also (ὃς καί)—as it is in immediate continuation further stated—went to the fight decorated with (*literally* "having," for "wearing") gold, like a girl. It can hardly be imagined that Nomion, the father, is referred to by ὅς :—*which* of the sons, then, is meant? A note in one of my copies of Homer says that *Amphimachus* "must" be the one intended; though without assigning any reason for such necessity. Both Pope and Cowper have awarded the distinction to him. Lord Derby has evaded the difficulty by treating the two brothers as a single person, unless his lordship alludes to the father by the demonstrative " he ":—

> " These came with Nastes and Amphimachus,
> Amphimachus and Nastes, Nomion's sons ;
> With childlike folly to the war he came,
> Laden with store of gold.". . .

Here his lordship has, in both places, reversed the order of the names as they stand in the text. This is the last mention of them there.

Νάστης 'Αμφίμαχός τε, Νομίονος ἀγλαὰ τέκνα,
'Ος καὶ χρυσὸν ἔχων πόλεμόνδ' ἴεν ἠΰτε κούρη.

The Homeric order of the names (as allowing, perhaps, the relative ὅς to be connected with the *last* named of the two conjoined brothers, and thus pushing aside the intervening father) appears to me the only reason for assigning to Amphimachus, as I have done, the unenviable preference. However, if he is wronged thereby, he won't *fight about* it; and with this pun upon his name (for which I hope to be pardoned) I now conclude my rambling notes.

THUS to his spouse illustrious Hector spake,
And stretch'd his arms his infant boy to take;
But the babe, screaming, turn'd his face away,
Affrighted at the terrible display
Of the fierce brazen helm with nodding crest,
And closely clung for refuge to the breast
Of his fair-girdled nurse : the parents smiled;
Then the fond father to appease the child,
Took from his head and laid upon the floor
The cause of dread; and the babe shunn'd no more
His sire, who kiss'd and dandled him, then pray'd :
    O Jupiter, and other gods ! he said,
Grant that my son may as distinguish'd be
Among the Trojans as myself;—that he,
In arms as pow'rful, may have the strength
To govern Troy, and that, whene'er at length
He shall return after successful war,
This praise, by thousands utter'd, he may hear :
" Lo ! Hector's son, who his sire far exceeds
In princely virtues and heroic deeds ! "

Then, too, the crimson spoils, pluck'd from the foe
Slain by his hand, let him for trophies show ;
While his fond mother, list'ning to the voice
Of her son's fame, shall feel her heart rejoice.
 Having so pray'd, he gave the darling boy
To his loved wife, who him, with tears of joy
And sorrow mingled, took, then fondly prest
The cherish'd infant to her fragrant breast.
The pitying husband her cheek still bedew'd
Stroked tenderly, and his discourse renew'd.

R. W.

Preparatory to adding a copy of the versions by Pope and Cowper
respectively of the same passage (which appears to have caused each of
them a great deal of trouble, as will be seen presently), I shall here insert
as close a translation of it as I can give, in prose ; in order that the three
metrical versions may be compared, and their respective degrees of fidelity,
or approximation to the original ascertained.

Thus having spoken, illustrious Hector with out-
stretched arms sought to take his son ; but the
boy, crying, turned back to the bosom of his well-
girt nurse, distressed at the aspect of his dear
father ;—fearing the brass and the crest of bristling
horse-hair, as he saw it nodding from the top
of the helmet. His loving father and venerable
mother laughed out [outright, or aloud]. Immediately thereupon illustrious Hector removed from
his head the glittering helmet, and placed it on
the ground. Moreover, when he had kissed his
son, and dandled him in his hands, he, praying
to Jupiter and the other gods, thus spake : " O

Jupiter, and ye other gods! grant that this my boy may become, as I am, distinguished among the Trojans; thus excellent in strength, and powerful to reign over Ilium; and that hereafter many a one (τίς) may say of him, returned from war, "Truly this man is greater than his father." May he bring back the bloody spoils from the foe by him slain [having slain his foe]; and may his mother in her heart rejoice! Having thus spoken, he placed his boy in the hands of his beloved wife, and she received him in her fragrant bosom, smiling tearfully. Her husband, perceiving it, pitied her,—gently stroked her cheek with his hand, and, calling her by name, said.

R. W.

NOTE. Εὔζωνος, which I have here translated "well-girt," and in my metrical version "fair-girdled," has, among these and other meanings, the signification of *full-bosomed;* and this term, perhaps, would be the most apt in the present instance, since the τιθήνη may be presumed to have been a *wet*-nurse.

Considering the sorrowful discourse to which the scene just described was an interlude, there seems to be an incongruity in the text by its representing the parents as "laughing out" at the alarm of the child—ἐκ δὲ γέλασσε πατήρ τε καὶ πότνια μήτηρ—I have therefore in my version substituted the word "smiled;" and a mournful smile would have been most in keeping. Cowper, however, says that "both parents smiled delighted," while Pope represents them as each smiling with *secret* pleasure, which is certainly more becoming the occasion of the sad meeting than laughing outright together.

"Venerable"--the usual rendering of πότνια—does not, according to our ordinary use of the word, appear to be a very appropriate term to apply to such a young woman as Hector's wife; but it may be taken in the sense of *honourable*, or the like, and as being applied to Andromache in reference not to her age, but to her rank and station, or her dignified character.

With a view to what I intend shall follow Pope's version, I find it convenient to give the precedence to Cowper's, though the later of the two.

The hero ended, and his hands put forth
To reach his boy; but with a scream the child
Still closer to his nurse's bosom clung,
Shunning his touch, for dreadful in his eyes
The brazen armour shone, and direful more
The shaggy crest that swept his father's brow.
Both parents smiled delighted; and the chief
Set down the crested terror on the ground:
Then kiss'd him, play'd away his infant fears,
And thus to Jove and all the powers above:

Grant, O ye gods! such eminent renown
And might in arms as ye have given to me,
To this my son, with strength to govern Troy.
From fight return'd, be this his welcome home—
" He far excels his sire "—and may he rear
The crimson trophy to his mother's joy.

He spoke, and to his lovely spouse consign'd
The darling boy; with mingled smiles and tears
She wrapp'd him in her bosom's fragrant folds,
And Hector, pang'd with pity that she wept,
Her dewy cheek stroked softly, and began.

COWPER.

Now I take the liberty of transcribing from an interesting biography
of Cowper, by the Rev. Canon Dale, prefixed to a new edition of Cowper's
Poetical Works, the following passage relating to his translation of
Homer:—.

" Among many pleasing circumstances which followed the appearance
of this translation, not the least gratifying to Cowper's affectionate heart
was the renewal of his long-suspended intercourse with the friend of his
early days, Lord Chancellor Thurlow. Homer furnished the subject of
this correspondence. Thurlow entertained doubts about the propriety of
translating Homer in blank verse, and sent Cowper two sheets full of
arguments in favour of rhyme, which he was to answer if he *could*. He

could and *did* so answer him as to convince the Chancellor that Homer might be best translated without rhyme—a result which afforded the poet no little satisfaction. ' Such,' he writes to his cousin and confidante, Lady Hesketh, ' is the candour of a wise man and a real scholar. I would to heaven that all prejudiced persons were like him! I answered his letter immediately, and here, I suppose, our correspondence ends.' Here, however, it did not altogether end. In 1793 Cowper resumed the subject in a letter to Hayley, comparing a translation of his own with Hayley's and Lord Thurlow's, of which he says, ' You, with your six lines, have made yourself stiff and ungraceful; and he, with his seven, has produced as good prose as heart could wish, but no poetry at all: a scrupulous attention to the letter has spoiled you both, you have neither the spirit nor the manner of Homer. A portion of both may be found, 1 believe, in my version, but not so much as I could wish.' In these words," resumes Canon Dale, "Cowper characterizes accurately his printed translation, as well as the passage itself, which we subjoin as the only specimen of his Homer's painting for which our limits will afford scope."

"O Jove! and all ye gods! grant this my son
To prove, like me, pre-eminent in Troy,
In valour such, and firmness of command!
Be he extoll'd, when he returns from fight,
As far his sire's superior! may he slay
His enemy, bring home his gory spoils,
And may his mother's heart o'erflow with joy."

" There is an ambiguity in the sixth line of this passage," continues Mr. Dale, " in reference to the pronoun *his*, which may mean either the gory spoils of the slain enemy, or of the young hero who has slain him. This would have been avoided by a close attention to the original; and accordingly it did not satisfy Thurlow, who repeated his objections, and this drew forth another and an improved translation."

" May all who witness his return from fight
Hereafter say, ' He far excels his sire,'
And let him bring back gory trophies stripp'd
From foes slain by him, to his mother's joy."

" On this Cowper observes, ' Imlac in Rasselas says, I forget to whom[1], " You have convinced me that it is impossible to be a poet." In like manner I might say to his lordship, You have convinced me that it is impossible to be a translator; on his terms at least it is, I am sure, impossible ; on his terms I would defy Homer himself, were he alive, to translate the " Paradise Lost " into Greek.' Yet even in the second

---

[1] This is a mistake of Cowper's: it is Rasselas who makes the remark to Imlac.

version," says Mr. Dale, "Cowper has overlooked the peculiar beauty and delicacy in the original. The translation would seem to imply that the mother of the young hero should rejoice in his having slain foes, and brought back gory trophies; and there is something incongruous in the association of maternal tenderness with exultation over fallen enemies. The original has nothing of the kind. The joy of the mother's heart is there called forth only by the safe return of her son."

It will be seen that in my translation I have escaped liability to the above censure; and this I did naturally, and without reference to Canon Dale's observation. The original, however, is silent as to the specific source of the mother's joy. In reference to this the words are simply— χαρείη δὲ φρένα μήτηρ : and, therefore, I think Mr. Dale is too positive in asserting that the mother's joy is called forth "only" by the son's return. Unfortunately for that assertion, the bringing home of the gory trophies is the last of the circumstances mentioned before the words just quoted from the text; and while I admit that it seems barbarous to single out that particular circumstance from the rest as the cause or the occasion of the joy, I am afraid that this feeling must, in fairness of construction, be ascribed to the *tout ensemble* of the case; therefore I consider myself to have been liberally indulgent to the delicacy contended for by thus compromising the question :—

> " While his fond mother, *list'ning to the voice*
> *Of her son's fame,* shall feel her heart rejoice."

I am equally surprised and pleased at having (since these lines were written) discovered that Pope has treated this incident in the same manner, though more beautifully, in his version, which follows :—

Thus having spoke, the illustrious chief of Troy
Stretch'd his fond arms to clasp the lovely boy.
The babe clung crying to his nurse's breast,
Scared at the dazzling helm and nodding crest.
With secret pleasure each fond parent smiled,
And Hector hasten'd to relieve his child ;
The glitt'ring terrors from his brows unbound,
And placed the beaming helmet on the ground.
Then kiss'd the child, and lifting high in air,
Thus to the gods preferr'd a father's pray'r.

O thou ! whose glory fills the eternal throne,
And all ye deathless pow'rs ! protect my son !
Grant him, like me, to purchase just renown
To guard the Trojans, to defend the crown ;
Against his country's foes the war to wage,
And rise the Hector of the future age !
So when, triumphant from successful toils
Of heroes slain he bears the reeking spoils,
Whole hosts may hail him with deserved acclaim,
And say, This chief transcends his father's fame,
While pleased among the general shouts of Troy,
His mother's conscious heart o'erflows with joy.
He spoke, and fondly gazing on her charms
Restored the pleasing burthen to her arms ;
Soft to her fragrant breast the babe she laid,
Hush'd to repose, and with a smile survey'd.
The troubled pleasure soon chastised by fear,
She mingled with the smile a tender tear.
The soften'd chief with kind compassion view'd,
And dried the falling drops, and thus pursued.

Cowper's trouble with the scene before us appears to have existed in the
difficulty of pleasing others ; Pope's, in that of pleasing himself. Those
who would like to see how his fair " creation rose out of chaos " may have
their curiosity gratified by inspecting the poet's rough draft, or " foul
copy," of the composition, in the British Museum, written on the back of
a letter directed, " To Mr. Alexander Pope at Mr. Screen's house at Bath,"
and franked " J. Addison." It exhibits the translator's perplexity in the
midst of rival ideas, and his difficulty of choice from among a variety of
competing words, the conflict ceasing sometimes in a word or phrase different from that which appears in print, and thus leading to the presump-
tion that the words in such cases eventually adopted were not finally
decided upon till the time of transcribing for the press, and then, perhaps,
in the very act of doing so ; when, consequently, there was no need of
making the original draft correspond. This, indeed, could not have been

very easily done ; since the jostling there of many successive interlineations, erasures, restorations, &c. (piled in many instances one over another in tiers, and presenting in some places an entanglement of imperfectly formed and staggering characters, apparently denoting impatience in the writer), had left scarcely a possibility of cramming in any further alterations. After all, this laboured performance suffers injury from three or four blemishes which might have been so easily avoided that it is wonderful how they could have escaped removal. In the ninth line—

" Then kiss'd the child, and lifted high in air "—

the pronoun *him* is wanting, but its insertion would have been incompatible with the metre of that line. The remedy, however, might have been found in substituting for " high in air " the words *him on high,* and the word *cry* for "pray'r" at the end of the next line. The couplet would then have read thus :—

" Then kiss'd the child, and, lifting him on high,
Thus to the gods preferr'd a father's cry."

The twenty-fourth line says that Hector

" Restored the pleasing burthen to her arms,"—

namely, to those of his wife : but he had received the child from the nurse, and, therefore, in handing him to the mother, did not "restore" him. The awkward twenty-sixth line, in addition to its oddity in speaking of " troubled pleasure chastised by fear," wants grammatical connexion with the next line. That oddity might have been prevented, and the proper connexion supplied in this way :—

" The joy thus felt *being* follow'd by a fear,
She mingled with the smile a tender tear."

But, in spite of its faults, the passage, on the whole, contains such beauties as may well atone for its extravagant divergences from the original.

Close Translation.

GODLIKE Achilles! think on thy father, of as great age as I :—both in the last gloomy stage of life [*quite literally*—on the pernicious threshold of old age]; and him, indeed, surrounding neighbours perhaps harass; nor [perhaps] is there any one to ward off [from him] war and ruin; and yet he indeed, hearing that thou art alive, rejoices in mind, and hopes every day [all the days] to see his beloved son returned from Troy. But I [am] most unhappy; for I begat most brave sons in spacious Troy : fifty I had when the Achæans came, and of them, I may say, none are left. Nineteen of them were from one womb [that of his consort]; but the others concubines brought forth to me in my palaces. Impetuous Mars slew [*literally*—loosed the knees of] most of them ; but he who was to me as 'twere the only one, and defended the city and them,—him, fighting for his country, thou lately hast slain. . . .

Hector ! . . . . for whose sake now I come to the
ships of the Achæans to redeem his corpse from
thee ; and I bring immense gifts.   But reverence
the gods, Achilles, and have compassion on myself,
remembering thy own father.   But I am yet more
pitiable than he : for I have borne such things as
no other mortal upon earth ever yet bore—to kiss
the hands of the slayer of my children [*literally*—
to reach to my mouth the hands, &c.].—R. W.

The same Versified.

Godlike Achilles ! on thy father think,
Equal with me in age ; both on the brink
Of gloomy Hades, while, perhaps, round him press
Some hostile neighbours, causing him distress,
And there is none at hand him to defend
Against the dangers that o'er him impend.
Still he is often cheer'd by the report
That thou'rt alive, and hopes for the support
And solace, yet, of his belovèd son,
When safe from Troy return'd, his warfare done.
But I am most unhappy ; for in Troy,
Ere the Achæans came, mine was the joy
Of then possessing fifty sons most brave,
Of whom alas ! none I may say I have.
Nineteen of these were from my consort's womb ;
Thirty-one others, in my royal dome,
By different concubines were brought to light,
And most of them has Mars despatch'd in fight.

But him who was as 'twere my only son,
Since my defence, and Troy's, lay in that one,
Combating lately on th' ensanguined plain,
For his loved country, thou thyself hast slain :
Yes, my son Hector ! wherefore to your feet ›
I venturing approach, with offerings meet,
This corpse to ransom.   Oh ! the great gods fear,
Achilles ; nor be thou to me severe.
Remember thine own father ; see in me
A father still more desolate than he :
For I have borne what other man ne'er bore—
To the paternal lips which thee implore
The hands stain'd with my children's blood to press,
And thus the author of my woes caress.

R. W.

Cowper's Version.

Think, O Achilles, semblance of the gods,
On thy own father, full of days like me,
And trembling on the gloomy verge of life.
Some neighbour chief, it may be, even now
Oppresses him, and there is none at hand,
No friend to succour him in his distress.
Yet, doubtless, hearing that Achilles lives,
He still rejoices, hoping day by day
That one day he shall see the face again
Of his own son from distant Troy return'd.
But me no comfort cheers, whose bravest sons,
So late the flower of Ilium, all are slain.
When Greece came hither I had fifty sons ;

Nineteen were children of one bed, the rest
Born of my concubines. A numerous house!
But fiery Mars hath thinn'd it. One I had,
One more than all my sons the strength of Troy,
Whom standing for his country thou hast slain—
Hector—his body to redeem I come
Into Achaia's fleet, and bring, myself,
Ransom inestimable to thy tent.
Oh, fear the gods, and for remembrance' sake
Of thy own sire, Achilles, pity me,
More hapless still! who bear what, save myself,
None ever bore, thus lifting to my lips
Hands dyed so oft with slaughter of my sons.

Pope's Version.

Ah! think, thou favour'd of the pow'r divine!
Think of thy father's age, and pity mine!
In me that father's reverend image trace,
Those silver hairs, that venerable face;
His trembling limbs, his helpless person, see!
In all my equal, but in misery!
But now, perhaps, some turn of human fate
Expels him helpless from his peaceful state;
Think from some pow'rful foe thou seest him fly,
And beg protection with a feeble cry.
Yet still one comfort in his soul may rise;
He hears his son still lives to glad his eyes;
And, hearing, still may hope a better day
May send him thee, or chase that foe away.

No comfort to my griefs, no hope remain,
The best, the bravest of my sons are slain !
Yet what a race; ere Greece to Ilium came,
The pledge of many a loved and loving dame.
Nineteen one mother bore—dead, all are dead.
How oft alas ! has wretched Priam bled !
Still one was left their loss to recompense,
His father's hope, his country's last defence.
Him too thy rage has slain ! beneath thy steel
Unhappy in his country's cause he fell !
For him through hostile camps I bent my way,
For him thus prostrate at thy feet I lay ;
Large gifts proportion'd to thy wrath I bear ;
Oh hear the wretched, and the gods revere !
Think of thy father, and this face behold !
See him in me as helpless and as old,
Though not so wretched : there he yields to me,
The first of men in sov'reign misery !
Thus forced to kneel, thus grov'ling to embrace
The scourge and ruin of my realm and race,
Suppliant my children's murderer to implore,
And kiss those hands yet reeking with their gore !

Upon this passage Pope makes the following remarks :—
" The curiosity of the reader must needs be awakened to know how
Achilles would behave to this unfortunate king : it requires all the art of
the poet to sustain the violent character of Achilles, and yet at the same
time to soften him into compassion.   To this end the poet uses no
preamble, but breaks directly into the circumstance which is most likely
to mollify him, and the two first [first two] words he utters are μνῆσαι
πατρός. 'See' [sic] 'thy father, O Achilles, in me.'   Nothing could be
more happily imagined than the entrance into his speech : Achilles has
every where been described as bearing a great affection to his father ; and

by two words the poet recalls all the tenderness that love and duty can suggest to an affectionate son.

" Priam tells Achilles that Hector fell in defence of his country. I am far from thinking that this was inserted accidentally; it could not fail of having a very good effect upon Achilles, not only as one brave man naturally loves another, but as it implies that Hector had no particular enmity against Achilles, but that, though he fought against him, it was in defence of his country.

" The reader will observe that Priam repeats the beginning of his speech, and recalls his [Achilles'] father to his memory at the conclusion of it. This is done with great judgment. The poet takes great care to enforce his [Priam's] petition with the strongest motive, and leaves it fresh upon his [Achilles'] memory ; and probably Priam might perceive that the mention of the father had made a deeper impression upon Achilles than any other part of his petition ; therefore, while the mind of Achilles dwells upon it, he [Priam] again sets him [the father] before his [the son's] imagination by this repetition, and softens him into compassion."

Does it not seem wonderful that the same perspicacity which dictated those judicious, but (especially in reference to the confusion of pronouns) rather loosely expressed remarks, did not enable the annotator to see that the language *he* (supposing him to be Pope himself), *not Homer*, puts into the mouth of Priam, in making him tell Achilles that his *rage* had slain Hector, and finally calling him a *murderer*, whose hands were *reeking* with the *gore* of the suppliant's children, was liable to counteract the softening tendency of the appeal to his filial piety and affection ? But in Homer there is nothing corresponding to any of these offensive terms.

In line twenty-five, it may have been observed, Pope uses the active verb *lay* instead of the neuter *lie*. How easy it would have been to avoid that error, thus :—

" For him before thy feet *myself* I lay."

Lord Derby has described this scene beautifully. Both Pope and Cowper represent Priam speaking of Hector as his *only* son ; and, according to the letter of the text, they were, perhaps, warranted in so doing ; though, as I take it, we should understand that, while he had actually lost many of his fifty sons, he had virtually and in effect lost them all, since, as I have put it in my version, his and the city's defence had lain in Hector now gone. Lord Derby seems to have taken a similar view of the case, as I am happy to find on referring to this part of his version whilst in the midst of writing the present paragraph. However, the fact is (if there are any facts in the case) that Priam's sons were not then *all* slain ; there being one, at least, and that a most remarkable instance of survivorship among those sons, in the person of Paris, who lived long enough to slay Achilles himself. This he did by shooting with an arrow the swift-footed hero whilst, in the temple of Minerva, he was engaged in wooing Polyxena (a daughter of Priam), with whom he had fallen in love. The arrow pierced the victim in his only vulnerable part—the heel by which his mother, Thetis, held him while dipping him in Styx, with the view of making him immortal : whereby she furnished an occasion for the only example I am aware of, in the English language, of imitating that Greek idiom which puts a neuter article with the infinitive mood of a verb for a cognate noun.

> " Not all the virtues of the Stygian lake
> Could save the son of Thetis from *to die ;*
> But that blind bard could him immortal make
> With verses dipp'd in dew of Castalie."

Thus we take leave of the bard, and of his hero.

MINOR TRANSLATIONS.

AUREUM MONITUM.

By Musonius.

Ἄν τι πράξῃς καλὸν μετὰ πόνου, ὁ μὲν πόνος οἴχεται,
τὸ δὲ καλὸν μένει·
Ἄν τι ποιήσῃς αἰσχρὸν μετὰ ἡδονῆς, τὸ μὲν ἡδὺ οἴχεται,
τὸ δὲ αἰσχρὸν μένει.

Translation.

If aught that's noble you achieve with pain,
The pain departs, the honour doth remain;
In aught that's base, though you should pleasure
find,
The pleasure dies, the shame remains behind.

RULE IN CASE OF DOUBT.

Bene præcipiunt qui vetant quidquam agere quod
dubites si æquum sit, an iniquum : Æquitas enim
lucet ipsa per se; dubitatio cogitationem significat
injuriæ. (*Cicero de Officiis.*)

Translation.

Well dictate they who bid you not to do
That which you doubt if it be right, or no :
For right doth shine with self-effulgent rays,
While doubt a sense of latent wrong betrays.

THE BOUNTY WHICH LEAVES THE BESTOWER
NONE THE POORER.

Homo qui erranti comiter monstrat viam,
Quasi de suo lumine lumen accendat facit :
Nihilominus ipsi lucet cùm illi accenderit.

ENNIUS.

Translation.

The man who courteously points out the way
To one who lucklessly had gone astray,
So acts as if he did in darksome night
From his own lamp give to another light ;—
No less he lights himself when he has lighted
A torch for him who was erewhile benighted.

ADDENDUM.

If you bestow part of your worldly store,
Less you possess than what you had before ;
But if you counsel or instruction give
To any of your brethren who live
In ignorance or error, none the less
Knowledge or wisdom do you still possess.

AN EXHORTATION TO PHILOSOPHY.

From the Greek of EPICURUS.

Let not the young philosophy postpone
Until to riper years they shall have grown ;
Nor let the old, however learn'd and wise,
Weary of lore, cease to philosophize ;
For none, let him be young or old, will find
Unseasonable a sound and healthy mind :
And he who says, " For me not yet's the time
To apply the mind to studies so sublime ;"
Or he who says, " For me it is too late
Learning and science still to cultivate,"
Resembles him who—youth or man—should say
It is too early, or too late a day
For the time, long or short, he may possess
That period to spend in happiness.

The Original.

Μήτε νέος τὶς ὢν μελλέτω φιλοσοφεῖν, μήτε γέρων
ὑπάρχων κοπιάτω φιλοσοφῶν· οὔτε γὰρ ἄωρος οὐδείς
ἐστιν, οὔτε πάρωρος πρὸς τὸ κατὰ ψυχὴν ὑγιαίνειν· ὁ
δὲ λέγων, ἢ μήπω τοῦ φιλοσοφεῖν ὑπάρχειν ὥραν ἢ
παρεληλυθέναι τὴν ὥραν, ὅμοιός ἐστι τῷ λέγοντι πρὸς
εὐδαιμονίαν ἢ μὴ παρεῖναι τὴν ὥραν, ἢ μηκέτι εἶναι.

THE WORTHIEST MAN, THE WORTHY MAN, AND THE WORTHLESS MAN.

In Imitation of HESIOD.

Among the worthiest of all mankind
Is he who, in a wise and virtuous mind,

K

Revolves the universal scheme of things,
Tracing them upward to their pristine springs,
And downward, thence, toward their destined end,
Pondering how all to greater good may tend;
And worthy he who doth the counsel heed
Of one whose worth and powers his own exceed;
But he's a worthless man, who's neither wise
Nor will the precepts of the prudent prize.

The Original.

Οὗτος μὲν πανάριστος, ὃς αὐτὸς πάντα νοήσῃ,
Φρασσάμενος, τά κ᾽ ἔπειτα καὶ ἐς τέλος ἦσιν ἀμείνω·
Ἐσθλὸς δ᾽ αὖ κἀκεῖνος ὃς εὖ εἰπόντι πίθηται.
Ὃς δέ κε μήτ᾽ αὐτὸς νοέῃ, μήτ᾽ ἄλλου ἀκούων
Ἐν θυμῷ βάλληται, ὅδ᾽ αὖτ᾽ ἀχρήϊος ἀνήρ.

NOTE. *Among the worthiest*] In saying "*among*" the worthiest, I have intentionally deviated from the original; thinking that, in doing so, I should be nearer the truth than in adhering closely to the text by saying, "he is the best of all," or "by far the best." Moreover, for the sake of uniformity of terms in the three degrees of comparison, I have translated *ἀχρήϊος* "worthless," instead of *useless*.

A PRECEPT.

In Imitation of "The Golden Verses" formerly (but erroneously, as it is now thought) ascribed to PYTHAGORAS.

Nightly, ere slumber on ~~your~~ thine eyelids fall,
Thy daily actions thrice to mind recall;
Inquiring of thyself, "Where have I been?
What have I heard there? what there have I seen?

What have I done, either of good or ill ?
What duty's task neglected to fulfil ?"
Beginning from the first, onward proceed,
Duly reflecting on each word and deed.
Then, if thou hast done amiss, afflict thy breast ;
If well, humbly rejoice, and peaceful rest.
Thee, acting thus, bright virtue will attend,
Guiding thy footsteps to a happy end.

Variations.

For the last two lines may be substituted either of the following
couplets :—

1.

These counsels followed will thy steps incline
To tread the path traced by the power divine.

2.

This rule, well practised, will thy footsteps guide
Where virtue and true happiness reside.

Literal rendering.

These . . . . will place thee in the footsteps of
divine virtue.

The Original.

Μὴ δ᾽ ὕπνον μαλακοῖσιν ἐπ᾽ ὄμμασι προσδέξασθαι,
Πρὶν τῶν ἡμερινῶν ἔργων τρὶς ἕκαστον ἐπελθεῖν·
Πῆ παρέβην ; τί δ᾽ ἔρεξα ; τί μοι δέον οὐκ ἐτελέσθη ;
Ἀρξάμενος δ᾽ ἀπὸ πρώτου ἐπέξιθι· καὶ μετέπειτα,
Δειλὰ μὲν ἐκπρήξας ἐπιπλήσσευ, χρηστὰ δέ, τέρπου.
Ταῦτα σε τῆς θείης ἀρετῆς εἰς ἴχνια θήσει.

THE STEP-CHILD AT THE TOMB OF HIS STEP-MOTHER.

An Epigram of CALLIMACHUS.

Στήλην μητρυιῆς πικρὰν λίθον ἔστεφε κοῦρος
ὡς βίον ἠλλάχθαι καὶ τρόπον οἰόμενος·
ἡ δὲ τάφῳ κλινθεῖσα κατέκτανε παῖδα πεσοῦσα·
φεύγετε μητρυιῆς καὶ τάφον οἱ πρόγονοι.

Translation.

As once a gentle boy a wreath arranged
Around the pillar of his step-dame's tomb,
Thinking her temper, as her life, had changed,
The pious offering provoked his doom.
For lo! the column falling kill'd the child,
And by that act this solemn warning gave:
Never expect step-mothers to grow mild;
Flee them, step-children, even at their grave.

The Translator begs leave to enter his protest against the too general condemnation of step-mothers. Judging from his own knowledge of a few, he thinks the exceptions to the supposed rule are not very uncommon.

EPITAPH.

From CALLIMACHUS.

Τῆδε Σάων ὁ Δίκωνος Ἀκάνθιος ἱερὸν ὕπνον
Κοιμᾶται· θνήσκειν μὴ λέγε τοὺς ἀγαθούς.

Translation.

Here doth Acanthean Saon, son of Dicon, lie
In sacred slumber: say not good men die.

INSCRIPTION FOUND ON A CENOTAPH IN MYSIA.

N.B. The asterisks denote the places of effaced letters. The apparent *gamma* at the beginning of the third line is the remainder of a *tau* that has lost its dexter arm.

MBOΣMENKPY
ΕΙΜΕΓΟΝΕΝΚΟΛΠ*
ΓΡΑΦΕΝΤΑ
ΝΟΜΑΜΕΝΠΤΟΛΕ
ΟΝΟΓΕΝΝΗΣΑΣΔΕ
ΣΕΛΕΥΚΟΣ
**ΝΤΑΕΤΗΣΔΙΚΟΜΗΝΛΙ*
ΕΣΔΟΜΟΝΟΙΔΕΓΟΝ
ΕΙΣ
ΜΥΡΟΝΤΑΙΚΕΝΕΑΙΣΕΛΠ*
ΣΙΤΕΙΡΟΜΕΝΟΙ
ΟΓΟΝΕΕΣΤΙΜΑΤΗΝΚΕ
ΝΕΩΠΡΟΣΨΥΧΕΤΕΤΥΜΒΩ
ΜΟΙΡΩΝΓΑΡΚΛΩΣΤΗΡΙΤΕΛ**
ΒΙΟΤΟΙΟΤΕΤΥΚΤΑΙ

The same metrically arranged, with the deficient letters supplied.

Τύμβος μὲν κρύπτει με τὸν ἐν κόλπῳ τραφέντα·
Τοὔνομα μὲν Πτολεμαῖον ὁ γεννήσας δὲ Σέλευκος·
Πενταέτης δ' ἱκόμην ἀϊδὲς δόμον· οἱ δὲ γονεῖς
Μύρονται, κεναῖς ἐλπίσι τειρόμενοι.
Ὦ γονέες, τί μάτην κενεῷ προσψύχετε τύμβῳ;
Μοιρῶν γὰρ κλωστῆρι τέλος βιότοιο τέτυκται.

A close Translation.

The tomb hides me, *after* having been nourished at the breast. Ptolemy my name, Seleucus begat me. At the age of five years I came to the dim abode. My parents lament, afflicted at the dis-

appointment of their hopes [by vain hopes].
Why, O my parents! in vain grow cold at my
empty tomb; for the thread [term] of my life was
spun [prepared] by the spindle of the Fates.

Paraphrase.

Me the tomb hides, once nourish'd at the breast
By a fond mother, lulling me to rest.
Son of Seleucus, Ptolemy my name,
When five years old I to Death's mansion came;
And my bereavèd parents now complain,
Afflicted at my loss—their hopes made vain.
Why, O my parents! linger at the tomb,
And shiver, while you mourn my early doom?
For by the Fates my thread of life was spun,
And by them cut when its short course was run.

TRANSLATIONS FROM MARTIAL.

The following beautiful Epigram, which, with my subjoined translation, is here introduced, I accidentally met with last night; when,
thinking it would make a suitable companion to the preceding Greek
Epitaph, I immediately put it into its English dress, which I hope, with
some diffidence, will not be thought to do much injustice to the original.
Those who understand the difficulty of accommodating rhymic metre to
proper names will not be too fastidious at the commencement.

It may not be impertinent to request the reader's attention to the
difference between the Greek child and the Roman one, in their respective
views of their similar fate. While the former remonstrates with his own
parents for their vain lamentation, the other begs even the casual reader
of the Epitaph to shed tears on his tomb.—September 15, 1869.

Conditus hic ego sum Bassi dolor, Urbicus, infans,
  Cui genus et nomen maxima Roma dedit.

Sex mihi de prima deerant trieteride menses,
  Ruperunt tetricæ cum mala pensa deæ.
Quid species, quid lingua mihi, quid profuit ætas ?
  Da lacrimas tumbo, qui legis ista, meo.
Sic, ad Lethæas, nisi Nestore serius, undas
  Non eat, optabis quem superesse tibi.

I, Urbicus, am hidden in this tomb,
  The son of Bassus, to whom mighty Rome
Gave name and lineage ; but I sorrow gave
  To him, unable infant-me to save.
Three years less by six months I numberèd,
  When the grim Fates ruptured my weak-spun thread.
What use my beauty, or my prattling tongue,
  Which could not coax them *that* life to prolong ?
Drop, reader, on my tomb some pitying tears :
  Thus, unless later than old Nestor's years,
May *he*, whom for survivor fain you'd save,—
  Your son—depart not to cold Lethe's wave.

TO A PROCRASTINATOR.

A close Imitation of MARTIAL's *Epigram to " Postume."*

To-morrow, Trifler, thou dost ever say,
Thou'lt live,—as live men *should*—nor more delay ;
But *that* to-morrow, tell me when it comes,
And in what place meanwhile it lurks or roams.
How distant is it ? whence must it be sought ?
Nay more—at what price can the same be bought ?

With Parthians and Armenians does it hide?
Or what new hindrance yet may it betide?
Priam's or Nestor's age it now attains;
And who can tell what more for it remains?
To-morrow liv'st thou? even to-day is late:
Yestern the wise ceased to procrastinate.

The Original.

Cras te victurum, cras dicis, Postume, semper.
Dic mihi cras istud, Postume, quando venit?
Quam longe est cras istud? ubi est? aut unde pe-
    tendum?
Numque apud Parthos Armeniosque latet?
Jam cras istud habet Priami vel Nestoris annos.
Cras istud quanti, dic mihi, possit emi?
Cras vives: hodie jam vivere tardum est:
Ille sapit, quisquis, Postume, vixit heri.

"The meaning is simple, and the point (apart from the philosophy of the
advice) is the common play on *cras* and *heri*, for which compare Pers. v.
67: 'Sed cum lux altera venit, Jam cras hesternum consumpsimus.'"
—See *Paley and Stone's "Epigrammata Selecta" of Martial.*
The Translator, by the words "as men *should*," which he has introduced into his version, merely expresses what is understood in the
original.

CONDUCEMENTS TO A HAPPY LIFE.

From the Epigram of M. Val. Martialis, *addressed to Julius
Martialis: amplified by the Translator.*

These are the things, my friend, that make life bless'd:
Sufficient wealth, by heritage possess'd,

Or legacy,—and not obtain'd by toil;
A farm of fair extent and fertile soil;
A cheerful, clean, and well-provided hearth [1],
That never either feels or fears a dearth
Of any thing that household wants require
In shape of either aliment or fire;
Freedom from law-suits, strife, and vain display
In the throng'd forum, or the public way;
Discreet simplicity, a tranquil mind,
With a frame healthy and robust combined;
A table plain, but yet set out with taste,
Where neither parsimony's seen, nor waste;
Pleased guests at times, and well-assorted friends,
With—what to happiness still nearer tends—
A sensible, kind, and virtuous wife,
To be your free companion for life;
Nights not intemperate, and from trouble free,
When sleep unbroken makes the dark hours flee,
The soul refreshing, till the morning ray
Brings to your waking eyes another day;
Not seeking to be other than you are,
While your last hour you neither wish, nor fear.

TRANSLATION OF COWPER'S "VOTUM."

Ye morning dews and health-renewing gales,
Ye groves, and pleasing shades in peaceful vales;

---

[1] *Focus perennis* are the only words in the original relating to the " hearth." My object in spinning them out into four lines was to express all the circumstances which I imagined to be included in the idea so tersely conveyed.

Ye grassy hills, and gladsome herbs on streams
Felicitous and bright in solar beams !
Oh that the fates to me would now renew
The calm delights which formerly I knew
In my paternal fields ; far off from fear,
Far off from guileful arts, from sordid care !
How would I wish—this which my ardent mind
Did ever hope in later years to find—
Before my own loved hearth tranquil and sage,
Unknown, to wait the steps of coming age ;
And then, my years being all—not sadly—flown,
Obtain at last green turf, or silent stone,
To guard my relics, and to mark the spot,
Till these should be decay'd, and I forgot.

I am not aware that either Cowper, or any one else, has ever made
a translation of his " Votum " previous to the above. Having examined
every copy I could find of his works, without meeting with any English
version of that piece, I venture here to insert my own.

TRANSLATION OF AN INSCRIPTION

On Sir Thomas More's Monument in the Old Church at Chelsea.

JOAN, the beloved pretty little wife
Of Thomas More *ere she had left this life,*
Lies here ; and I design this tomb to be
Likewise for ALICE, *now my wife,* and me.
The one, whom wedlock join'd in vigorous age,
Gave me a title to the parentage

Of one boy and three girls, who, living all,
Most duteously me their father call.
The other (praise of step-mother most rare)
Tends these step-children with as kind a care
As scarcely any mother e'er was known
To show to cherish'd offspring of her own.
Thus did the one, thus doth the other live
With me, who preference to neither give.
Whether THAT dearer was, or THIS is now,
Uncertain rests. Oh, how well here below
Could we have lived together, all the three,
Had so religion will'd, and destiny !
But since that could not be, let this be given :—
May the same tomb, may the same blissful heaven,
Unite us all, I pray :—then, *happy lot !*
Death will confer a boon which life could not.

The Original.

Chara Thomæ jacet hîc Joanna uxorcula Mori,
   Qui tumulum Alicæ hunc destino, quique mihi.
Una mihi dedit hoc, conjuncta virentibus annis,
   Me vocet et puer, et trina puellæ patrem.
Altera privignis (quæ gloria rara novercæ est)
   Tam pia quàm gnatis vix fuit ulla suis.
Altera sic mecum vixit, sic altera vivit ;
   Charior incertum est, hæc sit, an illa fuit.
O simul, O juncti poteramus vivere nos tres,
   Quàm bene si fatum religioque sinant.
At societ tumulus, societ nos, obsecro, cœlum !
   Sic Mors, non potuit quod dare vita, dabit.

The following memorandum may prove an interesting accompaniment to the foregoing Epitaph :—

It would have been gratifying to have been able to record that the concluding wish therein expressed had been wholly realized—viz. as to the terrestrial part of it, as we may well hope it has been in respect of the more important one. But of the mortal remains of this great and (in spite of his bigotry) good man, the headless trunk, only, rests in the vault at Chelsea. At his execution, in pursuance of the arbitrary, unjust, and cruel sentence passed upon him, in obedience to the dictates of the heartless and exasperated king, this ruthless tyrant became so indulgent as to remit the disgusting barbarities which in that age, and until within these few years, were the accompaniments to decollation, or hanging, for high treason ; but he could not extend his generosity so far as to dispense with the exhibition of the head upon London Bridge. After it had been there exposed for fourteen days (and, according to one account, blown off the spike into the Thames, whence it was rescued by a fisherman), it was obtained by More's daughter Margaret (the wife of Mr. Roper), who resolved to guard it as a precious relic during her life, and finally to have it buried with herself. In the mean time it was enclosed in a leaden casket; and—whether or not it was, previous to her decease, consigned to the vault of the Roper family in St. Dunstan's Church, Canterbury, to await her coming—there is, I believe, no reason to doubt that it was eventually placed in her arms, within her own coffin in that tomb.

It was through her intercession that his body, which had been buried in the Tower, was removed into the Chelsea vault.

MORS DECLINED.

On the Tombstone of a Schoolmaster in a Churchyard in Lincolnshire.

Mors mortis morti mortem nisi morte dedisset,
Æternæ vitæ janua clausa foret.

Translation.

Unless the death of death, to death,
The death by death had given,
Closed were the gate of endless life,
And man shut out from heaven.

WALLER'S TOMB.

This interesting relic, in Beaconsfield Churchyard, contains on its four sides six inscriptions in Latin, of which, it is hoped, the following lines will be considered a tolerably faithful translation. Their quaintest parts will be found the closest to the original.

EDMUND WALLER, to whom sacred is this stone,
Had for his birth-place, Coleshill, *hamlet lone ;*—
For place of study, Cambridge ;—for his father,
Robert ; and one of Hamden's stock for mother.
In the year sixteen hundred adding five,
On March the thirtieth, he began to live.
His first wife, Anna, was the only daughter
Of Edward Banks, and, *failing sons,* his heir.
By that first wife twice father he became,
And by his second thirteen times the same.
When twice five years he had survived this wife,
He reach'd the bourne of his own lengthen'd life,
And died the one-and-twentieth of October,—
Sixteen hundred eighty-seven the year.

Of EDMUND WALLER, what to death he gave
Lies buried in the silence of this grave.
Prince among all the poets of his time
(*Singing in numbers smooth, and tuneful rhyme*),
At fourscore years of age he still retain'd
The laureate wreath which in his youth he gain'd.
To him this praise his native language owes,
That—'tis a case allow'd you to suppose—

If e'er the Muses nine should cease to speak
The classic tongues of Latin and of Greek,
Whatever themes their numbers might rehearse
They'd love to express the same in English verse.

Traveller, alas ! thou viewest here the tomb
Where Edmund Waller finds the common doom ;
Who poet famous, with ancestral claims,
Standing distinguish'd 'mong the foremost names,
Himself devoted to the Muses' charms,
And to his country's cause 'mid fierce alarms.
Ere eighteen years of his long life were spent,
Sent up from Amersham to Parliament,
He held a seat with them who at the helm
Managed the arduous business of the realm.
This his life's tenor : nor, when old, was he
Wanting to duty, or from labour free.
He lived by people loved, by prince desired,
By one and all unceasingly admired.

In the same tomb with her late spouse most dear,
Mary his wife, of Bressy's race, lies here ;
Not less distinguish'd by her virtues rare,
Than for the numerous progeny she bare.
She thirteen times him a glad father made,
For they five sons and twice four daughters had ;
Whom all in turn having to this world given,
She, *ev'ry duty done*, return'd to heaven.

By this funereal marble, consecrate
To Edmund Waller and his second mate,
Most piously, to parents the most kind,
Edmund their son display'd his grateful mind.
To the well-meriting he has assign'd
The final honours by himself declined.

E. L., W. J., and F. H. G.
(*Whose names in full they do not let you see*),
According to the will and testament
Of the son Edmund, placed this monument,
In Julius Cæsar's month, the seventh number'd,
The year of Christ our Lord being seventeen
hundred.

Dr. Johnson, in his "Lives of the Poets," says, "Rymer wrote the inscription, and which I hope is now recovered from dilapidation." Many years have elapsed since that hope was expressed, but it has within the last seven years been realized, whatever neglect its object may have suffered in the interval.

The following account, with a view of the tomb and some of its surroundings, appeared in the *Illustrated London News*, January 17, 1863, Supplement :—

"The beautiful tomb at Beaconsfield, erected by his son to Edmund Waller the Poet, has at last been restored by Mr. Henry Harley, Statuary at Windsor, at the cost and pursuant to the directions of Mr. H. C. Waller, of Farmington, Gloucestershire, the Poet's descendant and representative; . . . and the tomb of black and white marble now stands out in all its pristine beauty—a magnificent memorial, well worthy of that admiration which Dr. Johnson bestowed upon it. The elegant Latin inscriptions, by Rymer of the Fœdera, are visible again, and the area round the tomb is repaired, embracing in its precinct the fine walnut-tree which overhangs the monument, and recalls the Wallers, an ancient and time-honoured family, that tree being their crest. The whole is a striking object, and combined with the tablets of Edmund

Burke, who was buried in the church close by, forms a double attraction to all who may wish to visit the shrines of the mighty dead."

After this, the Translator fears he would have been tantalizing some of his readers were he now to withhold the Latin inscriptions, which, therefore, are here presented.

EDMUNDUS WALLER, cui hoc marmor sacrum est,
Colshill nascendi locum habuit, Cantabrigiam studendi ;
Patrem Robertum, et ex Hamdenâ stirpe matrem.
Cœpit vivere 30 Martii, A.D. 1605.
Prima uxor Anna Edwardi Banks filia unica et hæres.
Ex primâ bis pater factus, ex secundâ tredecies,
Cui, et duo lustra superstes obiit 21 Octob. A.D. 1687.

EDMUNDI WALLER hîc jacet id quantum morti cessit.
Qui inter poetas sui temporis facile princeps,
Lauream quam meruit adolescens,
    Octogenarius haud abdicavit.
Huic debet patria lingua, quod credas,
Si Græcè Latinèque intermittent Musæ
    Loqui, amarent Anglicè.

Heus ! Viator, tumulatum vides Edmundum Waller,
Qui tanti nominis poeta, et idem avitis opibus,
Inter primos spectabilis, Musis se dedit et patriæ.
Nondum octodecenalis, inter ardua regni tractantes,
Sedem habuit, à burgo Amersham missus.
Hic vitæ cursus, nec oneri defuit senex, vixitque
    semper
Populo charus, principiis deliciis, admiratione omnibus.

Hîc conditur tumulo sub eodem
Rarâ virtute et multâ prole nobilis,
Uxor Maria ex Bressyorum familiâ,
Cum Edmundo Waller, conjuge charissimo,
Quem ter et decies lætum fecit patrem,
   V filiis et filiabus VIII.
Quos mundo dedit, et in cœlum rediit.

   Hoc marmore Edmundo Waller
Mariæque ex secundis nuptiis conjugi,
Pientissimis parentibus, piissime parentavit
   Edmundus filius.
   Honores bene merentibus dedit
   Quos ipse fugit.

E. L., W. I., F. H. G., ex testamento H. M. P.
   Me. Iulii 1700.

FROM THE ITALIAN OF METASTASIO.

The boatman welcomes with a smile
   The flatt'ring gale that fills his sail;
Not long: for in a little while
   The gale 's a blast that turns him pale.

The pilgrim loves the little cloud
   That shades him from the sun's fierce ray:
That cloud increased, with thunders loud,
   May shortly fill him with dismay.

If strong and promising appear
  To the fond dresser the young vine,
  At no fatigue does he repine
    To make it bear
    The expected fruit.
But the ungrateful tree he spurns,
  And sadden'd from it turns,
    If on its sunny bank
He find branches and foliage rank,
Of fruit and flower all destitute.

It is not love that guilty makes
  The soul where she an entrance finds,
And into shameful thraldom takes :—
  'Tis baneful passion there that binds.

To the condition of each breast,
  Whether it pure or vicious be,
Love, self-conforming, thence a test
  Derives of her own quality.

THE DANCING BEAR.

From the German [2].

A bear who long was forced to dance for bread,
Having at length broken his chain, and fled,

---

[2] I know not who is the author of this piece. I met with it in Rome, about thirty years ago. as an Appendix to a German Grammar.

Halted at the first friendly resting-place,
Where soon he was surrounded by his race,
Both males and females :—there while ursine misses
Were greeting their delighted guest with kisses,
And feeling in his presence very blest,
Their joy in roars throughout the woods exprest,
One brother-bear to another, as they roam,
Tells that lost Bruin is again at home.
Soon to the assembled throng Bruin related
The strange vicissitudes he had been fated
In foreign lands and cities to pass through,
And sufferings he was forced to undergo.
At last, his troubles o'er, as now he thought,
He boasted the accomplishments they had bought.
Of course the conversation turn'd on dancing,
When, with the view his merits of enhancing,
In dangling chain he on his hind-legs sprang,
And danced so well that the whole forest rang
With the applause of all the standers-by :
Such, for a short time was the ecstasy
Which Bruin's skill among his friends did raise ;
And quickly emulation follow'd praise.
His brother-bears, with vanity elate,
Essay'd beau-Bruin's steps to imitate,
But instantly experienced, to their woe,
That their bold effort was indeed "no go."
Scarcely could one of them e'en stand upright,
And on his back fell many an awkward wight.
The more, for that, did Bruin persevere
In making his own cleverness appear ;

And, consequently, ere he'd done so long,
Envy possess'd the late admiring throng.
" Be off," they cried; " away ! away with thee !"
" Fool ! would'st thou clever'r appear than we ?"
And then, in sooth, they chased away poor Bruin,
Whose vaunted talents thus produced his ruin.

Moral.

If thou art talented in any way,
Of thy abilities make no display.
Rather seem dull : they will not hate thee much,
Who think that, as themselves, thou too art such.
But, by so much as thou'rt than they more clever,
It thee behoves to manifest it never.
'Tis true that for a very little while
Thy skill may gain for thee a favouring smile.
Still trust not; boast not even of to-morrow;
For envy thy success will surely follow,
Converting thy undoubted excellence
Into an irremissible offence.

Postscript by the Translator.

Fain the Translator would here nullify
So foul a blot upon humanity :
But to deny all ground for such a charge
Were to assume a latitude too large.
Yet, while of excellence no vain display
Should e'er be made, 'twould be absurd to say

That, on account of the dull envious crew,
Your useful talents should be kept from view.
Nay, more : *so let your light before men shine*
That they may glorify its source divine,
Stands a commandment on the sacred page,
And ought to be observed in every age.
Ye, then, who have ability and skill
To instruct and please, your mission still fulfil ;
Still let the painter and the poet show
The taste and fire that in their spirits glow ;
Spread o'er the canvas, stamp upon the page,
Charms that the fancy and the heart engage.
While sage and moralist their efforts use
More generous feelings in base minds to infuse ;
Each one persuading his less brilliant brother
Envy and hatred in the breast to smother :
For, though not every one's by genius fired,
He yet may learn to make himself admired
By the possession of some quality
That shall the lack of brighter parts supply.

THE PILGRIM.

From the German of SCHILLER.

Still frolick'd I in life's gay spring,
    When restless I resolved to roam,
The sports of youth relentless leaving,
    And scenes of my paternal home.

My birthright—all I could command—
Cheerful and trustful I resign'd,
And, grasping light the pilgrim's wand,
I sallied forth with childlike mind:

For a mighty hope impell'd me,
And a prophetic, mystic voice,
Exclaiming, " Go ! the way 's before thee,
Towards the East : be that thy choice :

" Aye, eastward, till a golden portal
At length thou reach ; there enter thou ;
For what's earthly here, and mortal,
Heav'nly and fadeless there will glow."

Evening came, in turn came morning,
And never, never did I tire ;
Yet still remain'd, my fond chase scorning,
Conceal'd the goal of my desire.

Hills beyond hills before me stood,
And streams hemm'd in my ceaseless march ;
A bridge I built across each flood,
Over each chasm I flung an arch ;

And to a river's bank I sped
That, rapid, flow'd towards the East ;
Fearless, and trusting to its thread,
I threw me on its wavy breast

Onward, into a boundless sea,
   It bore me, never to return;
Now empty space spreads all around me :
   No nearer am I to the bourne.

Thither no path leads hence away :
   Ah! the bright heaven, that seem'd so near,
Will never touch this world's dull clay :
   The wish'd for *there* is never *here !*

THE IDEAL.

From the German of SCHILLER.

Thus wilt thou faithless from me part,
   With every pleasing fantasy ?
With all thy joys, and all thy smart,
   Wilt thou inexorably flee ?
Can nought thy glitt'ring stream detain,
   Oh thou, my life's loved golden prime ?
It rushes—ah ! entreaty's vain—
   Into the sea that swallows time.

Quench'd is that sun whose rays, evolved
   Upon youth's path, my fancy warm'd,
The ideal visions are dissolved
   With which the inebriate heart was charm'd.
The sweet belief has pass'd away
   In things wherewith my young dream teem'd,
To rough reality a prey,
   What once divine and beauteous seem'd.

As whilom, pining with desire,
　Pygmalion press'd to his fond breast
The sculptured stone, it glow'd with fire
　That sensibility exprest;
So I my arms of love did wreathe
　Round nature's form with youthful glow,
Till she began to warm, to breathe
　Against my heart, and poet's brow.

Partaking then my rapt'rous bliss,
　The lovely mute a language found;
And while she gave me back a kiss,
　Joyful, I felt my heart rebound.
Then lived to me the tree, the flow'r,
　Then sang to me the lapse of streams,
And things that own no sense's pow'r
　Responded to my voice of dreams.

The narrow breast, with gen'rous strife
　To encircle all within its bound,
Expanded,—swelling with fresh life,
　In word and act, in form and sound.
How grand and noble this world seem'd
　While still its folds the germ conceal'd!
How small, how mean, by me 'tis deem'd
　E'er since its leaves have been reveal'd!

With what a bold, undaunted air—
　Happy in dreams where all he view'd
Was fair, and free from sordid care—
　The youth life's untried course pursued

Till as to Æther's palest star
  His project's flight him upwards bore,
Nought was too high, and nought too far,
  For th' unwearied wing to explore.

What object e'er seem'd hard to attain
  By him essaying glorious deeds ?
How buoyant did life's car maintain
  Its course, as drawn by airy steeds !
Convoy'd by Love with rosy flame,
  And Fortune with her golden wreath,
And with a starry crown loud Fame,
  And radiant Truth of heavenly breath.

Ah ! those companions of my way,
  Ere half was travell'd disappear'd ;
And I was left forlorn to stray,
  Prey to a fate I ne'er had fear'd.
Her light-wing'd flight first Fortune sped,
  Knowledge her thirst could never quench,
And clouds of gloomy doubt o'erspread
  Truth's radiant orb that ne'er did blench.

I saw Fame's sacred wreath of bay
  Upon the vulgar brow profaned ;
And ere had ended my life's May,
  Love's rosy days to me had waned !
More and more still and lonely grew
  My journey o'er the roughen'd way,
And Hope scarce one pale gleam e'er threw
  To save the wanderer from dismay.

Of all the throng, who is the guide
  Whose constant steps my path now tend ?
Who the consoler at my side
  Whose solace but with life will end ?
Thou, Friendship, of the tender hand,
  That gently heals each mental wound ;
Of all life's burdens thou the band
  Dost loosen :—thee I've sought and found.

And thou too fondly dost conspire
  With her the soul-storm's rage to still,—
Employment, thou who ne'er dost tire,
  Whose gentle action works no ill.
True, thou'rt a sand-grain in amount
  When vast Eternity appears
Contrasted; yet from Time's account
  Canst strike out minutes, days, and years.

Variation.

True, thou art but a grain of sand
  Beside eternity's vast pile ;
Yet canst thou with thy magic wand
  Time of his heavy debt beguile.

THE FUTURE, THE PRESENT, AND THE PAST.
Translation of SCHILLER's *" Sayings of Confucius."*

The steps of time are of three different kinds :
The future slow, as moving without will ;
The present's foot no resting-place e'er finds ;
The past alone standeth for ever still.

Impatience can't induce time to increase,
However slow he seems, his coming pace;
No fear, or doubt, can ever make him stay,
When on his parting course he flies away.
Deaf to repentance and the enchanter's strain,
The past, as now, for ever will remain.

Would'st thou end happily, be timely wise:
With the slow future prudently advise;
But while its counsels thou may'st well receive,
Never thy work to its performance leave.
Choose not for friend that which flies fast away,
Neither for foe that which must ever stay.

NOTE. This translation (which is almost literal) corresponds stanza for
stanza, and line for line, with the original; the rhymes of which, also, are
in the first stanza alternate, and in the other stanzas in couplets.

The same observation, so far as it relates to the correspondence of
stanzas, is likewise applicable to the preceding pieces from Schiller.

ENCOURAGEMENT.

From the German of ANNA VON KEISSENBERG.

Wherefore, fond man, pursue with panting breath,
   And aching brow, an ever distant good?
Luck will not crown thee with the conqu'ror's
   . wreath:
Proudly renounce her, then, with daring mood.

Cease from th' unequal contest, full of pain,
  In which the weary soul but wastes her powers ;
For never, ah ! by striving wilt thou gain
  Aught that a god himself not freely showers.

As the bland hov'rings of a pleasing dream
  The placid sleeper uninvoked attend,
So too, unsought, must Fortune's golden stream
  From her bright star to this dull earth descend.

Flee to the silent depths of thy own soul ;
  Follow a star whose radiance is more mild ;
And then, however thy hard fate may scowl,
  To it at length thou shalt be reconciled.

This star is Faith, fix'd firm on holy might ;
  To her be thou indissolubly bound :
She'll guide thee safe in storm and darkest night
  Though under thee should quake the troubled
    ground.

Then, too, Faith's sister-star shall brightly shine,
  And light thee onward with her cheering rays ;
While Faith and Hope with Peace shall intertwine,
  And blessed shalt thou live and end thy days.

Yes, Peace after suffering shall, like heaven's soft dew,
  Descend on thee ; and, lastly, round thy grave,—
When friends have there pronounced the fond
    adieu,—
Shall endless peace over the green turf wave.

GOD'S GOODNESS.

From the German of CHRISTIAN FÜRCHTEGOTT GELLERT.

How great is the Almighty's goodness !
Is he a man whom it not moves ?
Who stifles in a heart that's heedless
The gratitude which him behoves ?
Let God's great love rightly to measure
My supreme duty ever be ;
Nor let my heart forget Him ever,
Who never has forgotten me.

Who has me wond'rously constructed ?
The God who had of me no need :
Who has with patience me conducted ?
He, whose counsels oft I've fail'd to heed.
Who in my conscience peace instils ?
Who to my spirit new strength lends ?
My prosperous cup of life who fills ?
His hand it is that all good sends.

Beyond the scenes by this world bounded,
Behold, my soul thy destined state,
Where thou, with excellence surrounded,
God, as He is, wilt contemplate.
These joys are thine by title sure,—
God's goodness undeserved and free :
Lo ! to this end had Christ to endure
Death, that with Him we blest might be.

Shall I this God, then, not revere,
Nor more His kindness seek to know ?
Shall He me call, and I not hear ?
The path He shows shall I not go ?
Let in my heart His word be graven,
Me inwardly His will approve,—
Love above all things God in heaven,
And, as myself, my neighbour love.

This, thanks to Him, this is His will,—
That I be perfect made as He :
So long I that command fulfil
His image is renew'd in me.
If in my heart His love shall dwell,
Though oft, from weakness, I may fail,
To ev'ry duty 'twill impel,
Nor over me shall sin prevail.

Grant that Thy love and goodness, Lord,
Ever before my sight may be,
That they fresh impulse may afford
To dedicate my life to Thee.
Solace in pain let them impart,
In times of wealth my steps attend,
And, lastly, conquer in my heart
All terror of my coming end.

In an " Evangelisches Gesang-Buch " which I purchased in Germany
in 1842, the second line of the first verse expresses a negative, " Der
ist kein Mensch den sie nicht rühret : i. e. *He is no man whom it moves
not.*" But in Professor Max Müller's German Classics the interrogative
form is used thus :—*Ist der ein Mensch den, &c. ?* And this I have
followed, as being, in my opinion, the preferable reading.

ORIGINAL PIECES.

ORIGINAL PIECES.

SONNET

Addressed to a Young Friend, in reference to the saying, " There is a right way and a wrong one for every thing."

Unnumber'd are the ways of going wrong,
　One only way there is of going right;
　Choose thou this way, keeping thy end in sight,
Whether thou walk alone, or in a throng.

Throughout thy journey, be it short or long,
　May truth and faith unceasingly unite—
　Pillar of cloud by day, of fire by night—
To guide thy footsteps and preserve thee strong

Against all ills, till thou shalt reach the strand
　Where error's mazes never more perplex
　The weary traveller o'er this world's rough road,
Nor anxious cares and doubts his spirit vex,
　But cheerful sunbeams gleam across the flood
　Wooing his passage to a happier land.

M

SONNET

Occasioned by the fact therein related.

A farmer [1] lay in bed with broken spine,
Caused by his fall from a high load of hay ;
And he, though conscious he was near the day
When he his long-used sickle must resign
To the great reaper Death, did not repine ;
But calmly bade his wife and sons to lay
His frame, when lifeless, where the solar ray
That gilds the corn-fields, on his grave should shine.
Thus, spite of reason, fancy's plastic pow'r
With unrealities surrounds man's doom,
Blending with the oblivion of the tomb
Feelings that vanish with his final hour.
"Choose me a sunny place," the dying farmer said,
And in a sunny spot, now dead, he's peaceful laid.

EL PERTURBADO.

Written, on a gloomy day, for a lady's Album, which was prefaced with
a request that none of the contributors to it would insert therein any
thing not in accordance with the tenor of their own thoughts.

Ah ! if my present strain in sooth must be
Accordant with the tenor of my thoughts,
My lady fair, you will not hear from me
A joyous song, but one of mournful notes.

---

[1] One of my own tenants.

For I am subject to a mystic pow'r,
   That, wheresoe'er I either go or stay,
Midst present scenes points to a coming hour,
   And calls my thoughts to objects far away;—

Presenting contrasts to each phase of joy,
   And with all projects fond, for future bliss,
Mingling forebodings vague of sad alloy,
   Which I in vain endeavour to dismiss.

Thus, when, perchance, joining the festive board,
   I mix my voice with sounds of mirth and glee,
And when some fair hand wakes the tuneful chord,
   My soul doth thrill at the sweet minstrelsy;

Even midst these scenes that bid the heart rejoice,
   And kindle lustre in the laughing eye,
Into my mental ear a secret voice
   Whispers, "How soon these witching pleasures die."

Then while the hall's resplendent with the blaze
   Of festal lamps, I see them fade away,
And flexile forms threading the dance's maze
   To me appear transform'd to rigid clay.

Quitting anon the scenes where pleasure flaunts,
   I tread fair nature's walks, and breathe the air,
In rural spots, where meditation haunts,
   But here such thoughts pursue as met me there.

When spring doth clothe with leaves the forest trees,
And in the verdant meads the flow'rets blow,
I see those leaves scatter'd by autumn's breeze,
I see those meadows clothed in winter's snow.

Now, gentle lady, whensoe'er you see
An autumn leaf borne on the moaning wind,
View in that leaf an emblem sad of me,
And sing a requiem to my troubled mind.

These verses are inserted out of the order of time in which they were
written, in order that they may appear in juxtaposition with the next
piece, written some years later.

EL TRANQUILIZADO.

No more shall moody fancies haunt
My now released and tranquil mind :
Ye gloomy phantoms all, avaunt !
In me a master now you'll find.

What, though the festive board no more
Inspire my heart with mirth and glee,
And though " my dancing days are o'er,"
More solid pleasures wait on me.

My books, my pen, my garden—all—
Surround me, with my *other* friends ;
Pleasures are these that never pall,
That for the past make rich amends.

Oh, may it please the Power benign
These to continue whilst I am here!
And may I calmly them resign
When I must go . . . . I know not where.

A PARADOX.

Cum sitis similes, paresque vita,
Uxor pessima, pessimus maritus,
Miror non bene convenire vobis.

MARTIAL.

Paraphrase.

By a JUSTICE OF THE PEACE.

Supposed to be addressed by him to a pair of the above description, on the occasion of their appearing before him on reciprocal charges of assault and battery.

If true the proverb is, that " like likes like [2],"
I wonder that you two each other strike :
Alike your tempers, and alike your lives,
The worst of husbands, and the worst of wives,
Such an exceedingly well-match'd pair
Ought to draw cheek by jowl, like horse and mare ;
Whereas—so adverse are your ways, alack !—
Though equally, like pot and kettle black,
You either sit apart to rail and glump,
Or, meeting, one another bump and thump.
The ruffian pot, when 'tis his turn to bubble,
Swears married life is full of toil and trouble ;

Similis simili gaudet.

The vixen kettle, when she ought to sing,
Cries, " Oh, had I never seen a wedding-ring ! "
And thus the state that was design'd to bless,
Is made a scene of ceaseless wretchedness.
This time, however, I will let you go :
Go home in peace ; but, at the same time, know,
The one that doth the other next assail
Shall find a peaceful home in Gloucester jail.

CHARADE.

My whole has twelve parts ; and its first six form
The name of object ne'er, in breeze or storm,
Despised by sailor voyaging from far,
In the bold ship of commerce or of war
Near treach'rous shores, where oft some hidden rock
Gives the incautious keel a fatal shock.
Of the other six parts, the last five read,
And forthwith to your mental view will spread
A scene where cattle graze, or harvests wave,
And where, sometimes, the warrior finds a grave.
But 'twixt the sep'rate six and five doth rise
A form which bounds all bliss, and ends all sighs :
Though serpentlike, it links in friendly band
Those that erst stood aloof on either hand.
This union strange now constitutes a name
Blazon'd not dimly on the roll of fame.
The name is mine,—a place the Muse holds dear,
And which the patriot ever must revere :

For whilom sang among my verdant glades [3],
Pellucid lakes, coy streams, and sylvan shades,
As sweet a bard as ever did compose
Sonnet to "Lady fair," or "Lovely Rose."
There, too, more late, a senator, renown'd
For eloquence and taste, a refuge found,
From the turmoil and din of party strife,
In the amenities of rural life;
And in the precincts of my hallow'd fane
The Statesman's dust, and Poet's doth remain.
For ever is that Poet's lute unstrung,
Senates no more shall hear that statesman's tongue;
But now [4] a famed and living statesman's DAME
Enjoys a noble title in my name;
And HIS, recorded on the historic page,
Shall last to Albion's remotest age.

SCRAPS ABOUT THE PAINS AND PLEASURES
OF MEMORY.

"THE BIT OF SPANISH" which haunted the Author of
"Companions of my Solitude."

Cuan presto se va el placer,
Como despues de acordado
Da dolor;

---

[3] *Verdant glades,* &c.] Such I believe is the present description of —— Park,
the Poet's seat two hundred years ago. Of the late Statesman's once splendid mansion
and grounds not a vestige remains; the former having been destroyed by fire about
twenty years after his decease, and the latter having lost their traces in the farming
fields of which they now form part.

[4] In 1869.

Como al nostro paracer
Qualquier tiempo pasado
Fué mejor.

Free Translation.

How soon, alas ! does pleasure pass away !
Nor tears, nor prayers prevail to make her stay :
She seems to come only forthwith to go,
And, by departing, aggravate our woe ;
So that of all times which are past and gone
Any to us seems better than the one
Which the departed pleasure to us gave :
How to delusion is the mind a slave !

N.B. The last line is added, not more for the sake of rhyme than
as a protest against the opinion expressed in the lines preceding ; the
Translator coinciding with the author alluded to, and with Sydney Smith,
in the sentiment that " the remembrance of past pleasure is present
pleasure."

A bald rendering of the Spanish is merely this :—

How soon pleasure departs !
How after being granted
It gives pain !
So that in our opinion
Any time past
Was better.

This, having reminded me of the exclamation in Blair's " Grave "—

" Of joys departed
Not to return, how painful the remembrance !"

—led me to compose the following

SONNET.

That joys departed never can return
   Is certainly a melancholy thought;
   But that their memory with pain is fraught
Is an assertion we may justly spurn.

None can deny—for 'tis a truth most stern—
   That vicious pleasures leave to memory nought
   But keen remorse, that makes them dearly bought;
Which many, by experience only, learn.

While of true pleasures all that doth decay
   Is the corporeal or grosser part;
   Their spirits in the memory and heart
Still, still survive; nor does affliction's day,—
   Whate'er of ill therein may supervene,—
   Cause us to wish those joys had never been.

Hereupon, by a natural concatenation of thoughts, there came to my
recollection a pleasure which, four-and-twenty years ago, in the Hofburg
Theatre at Vienna, I experienced on hearing a very charming actress in
a Schauspiel called "Selbst-Beherrschung," of which the only expression
I remembered was the sentence about to be prefixed, as a motto, to the
following lines, which sprang from the seminal idea contained in it.

THE BOUQUET OF MEMORY.

Doch will ich noch, je und je, am verwelkten Strauss der
Vergangenheit riechen.

What though few wayside flowers fresh-springing
   bloom,
As I pursue my journey to the tomb,   ·

Wither'd parterres waft on fond memory's gale,
A fragrance which I gratefully inhale,
Causing my drooping spirits to revive
As I in pleased imagination live
With friends gone long before me to repose,—
Gone like the fragrant lily, or sweet rose !
Friends of whom some were early snatch'd away,
As spring-flowers pluck'd, or mown as summer hay ;
Me leaving, like sere leaf, for autumn's fall,
Or spared for winter's blast, that scatters all
Which frost untimely, blight, or slow decay
Through seasons past, till then, allow'd to stay.
Calmly my turn I wait : let there be " light
At evening-tide ;" then welcome peaceful night.
To the cold urn shall spring her visit pay,
On the grave's night shall dawn eternal day [5].

VERSES

On my Crest, a stag couchant, pierced through the neck by an arrow ; with motto, " UTERE DIE.*"*

The fleetest stag that ever ranged
   Through forest wild or vista'd park,
How oft soe'er his course be changed,
   Must meet at length the destined mark.

---

[5] " But when shall spring visit the mould'ring urn ?
Ah ! when shall it dawn on the night of the grave ?"
                             The Hermit, by BEATTIE.

'Tis not alone when hounds pursue,
  And hunters follow in their train,
Barking and shouting loud halloo!
  That he's in danger to be slain.

When in the leafy copse he hides,
  Couch'd on the verdant turf at rest,
While zephyr fans his panting sides,
  The arrow sly may pierce his breast.

And thou, O man! though safely past
  Through scenes of tumult and of strife,
When enter'd on repose at last,
  In sad surprise may'st close thy life.

Then what thy hands shall find to do
  Accomplish duly with thy might;
Nor let thyself, or others, rue
  Thy sloth when on thee steals life's night.

In time of health "use thou the day,"
  Nor, thoughtless, for sick hours postpone
What duty bids; but watch and pray
  That all thy doings be well done.

So, when thy final hour is near,
  The angel's [6] voice may whispering say,
" Good servant, quit thy work, nor fear,
  For well hast thou employ'd thy day."

---

[6] The word "angel" is here used in its primitive sense of *messenger*.